HEALING THE ORC'S HEART

TROLLKIN LOVERS BOOK TWO

LYONNE RILEY

Copyright © 2023 by Lyonne Riley
All rights reserved.

Cover art by Rowan Woodcock
Cover design by Haya in Designs
Interior spot illustrations by Laura Spicer

No part of this book may be reproduced in any form or by any electronic or mechanical means, including information storage and retrieval systems, without written permission from the author, except for the use of brief quotations in a book review.

Introduction

When Blizzek is conscripted to fight in the war against the humans, he assumes he'll end up dead—that's the only possible outcome for a stubborn, arrogant orc like him. But when he's gravely injured in a battle, it's a human woman with gentle, brown eyes who saves his life.

Nera inherited her skills as a healer from her father, who always taught her to care for the sick, no matter who they were. When she finds an orc out in the woods, well, she has a duty to help him. But is it more than just duty that convinces her to bring him home with her and nurse him back to health, too?

While kind Nera cares for him day after day, Blizzek finds an unspoken desire slowly blooming between them. But their people are at war, and Blizzek must return to the front lines, or die as a deserter—which would mean leaving Nera forever.

CONTENT WARNINGS

- *War and violence*
- *Graphic depictions of sex*
- *Captivity and slavery*
- *Physical assault*
- *Breeding*
- *Pregnancy*

CHAPTER 1

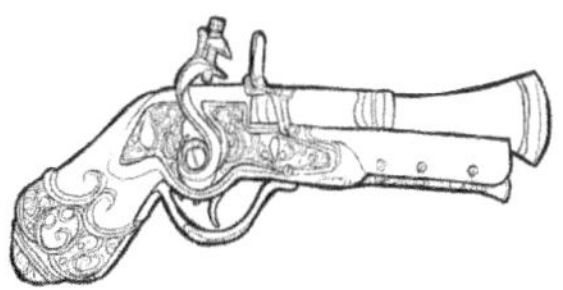

BLIZZEK

I assume I'm dead.

When the shrapnel bomb hit, I was a hundred paces away. Shards of metal flew in every direction in a whirlwind of deadly steel. My body was turned to one side when it landed, so I got two pieces in my side, another in the thigh, and the rest scattered across my hip and shoulder. The impact alone was enough to throw me to the ground.

All around me, trollkin are screaming. The bomb landed in the center of our ranks, and my unit is lying on the ground everywhere, moaning and bleeding and dying. My head is throbbing, pounding in my skull. Every part of my body feels like it's on fire.

This damned war.

I didn't want to come here and become fodder in this massacre. I was minding my business, having a pint at the local watering hole, wondering what had become of my best friend.

That's who he was, really. I'd grown accustomed to traveling with Raz'jin, the blue-skinned troll with a peculiar appetite. But something had ruined him: A human. He chose her without even realizing it. They had bonded across language barriers. But after her, something inside him broke, and he had no more will to live. I wasn't surprised in the least when he joined the war effort. He had decided dying was the easier option.

I, on the other hand, am an orc who enjoys living. I'm not bound by idiotic things like *mating*. I make my coin where I can, I fuck beautiful trollesses and orcesses when I come across them—which is frequently, especially in the sprawling city of Kalishagg—and I keep my hide clean. I don't start fights I can't win, and becoming a pawn of the Great Chieftain in his quest to destroy humankind is not a fight you generally come back from.

At least, I didn't start fights before the conscription. That was when I knew I couldn't run from it anymore, and I'd be joining that idiot Raz'jin out on the battlefield. Just another orc throwing my life away.

I didn't wait to be dragged in. I signed up that day, grabbed my faithful blunderbuss and my gear, and got on the next wagon headed north toward war.

Being on the front lines had changed Raz'jin, and I saw my future in him. I've been destined to die in this war from the beginning, so finding myself here now, swimming in pain, is something I expected. My side riddled with shrapnel of broken armor and shards of sword? That's a little more unexpected. The humans are clever, I have to give them that, for using our own dead soldiers against us.

The sound of voices rises over the groans of agony all around me. If I can hear the humans, that means I'm still a little bit alive. And there's no way I came out here to be butchered while I lie there helplessly.

The sky is darkened with dust and smoke. The settlement's wooden walls are aflame, with humans all around trying to put it out. Good for us—we managed one small victory here, at least. If they can't put the fire out, the walls will fall. I've just got to figure out how to get as far from the action as possible.

I'm at the very edge of the woods, and nearby I can see one of the others in my unit lying on the ground, moaning. I try to sit up enough to get one of my legs under me, but the shrapnel lodged in my side screams in complaint. The voices are growing closer. I only have one choice.

My good side on the ground, I start dragging myself a few inches at a time away from the bright orange light of the flames. Night is setting in, and if I can just find my way into the darkness of the woods, I'll be much harder to find.

Everything in my body is burning as I pull and pull—elbow first in the dirt, then dragging the rest of my body along with it. I slow down once I'm under the cover of trees to catch my breath. A long trail of blood follows my path along the forest floor. I'll be easy to track in the light of day, so I had better make myself scarce and try to get back to camp before then.

If I'm honest with myself, there's no way I'll make it before I bleed out. But there's one thing we orcs were made to do: Push through. We were blessed with sturdy bodies, tough skin, and an unmatched will. Where there's an orc, there's a way, and I won't forget that.

And so, with what strength remains in my body, I pull and pull myself across the forest floor. The screams of my countrymen and my enemies both fade as I get deeper into the trees, away from the bloodshed, shrapnel, and fire.

I don't know how much time passes. It's when the sun

starts to rise again and the sky fills with color that my orc will finally gives out.

Nera

They told me not to stay. But this is my home, where Refiel and I had built our lives together. This little house, the sprawling garden, the shed, and the sheep pasture—it's all I have left of him.

The war is getting closer every single day. I can hear the gunshots and the screams way off in the distance. I see the smoke rising into the sky as other human cities are burned to the ground.

Without Refiel, there's no reason to be afraid. If I die here under a trollkin's blade, then I die here, and I'll finally join him in the afterlife, whatever that is.

Tonight's battle is closer than it's ever been before. I hear explosions, and the acrid smell of burning wood and flesh fills my nose when I step outside the house. My sheep hide under their shelter, shaken by the sounds of war.

All I can think about as I listen are the dying and the dead. How many humans and how many trollkin have already fallen, and for what? Just like my Refiel, they're all blood sacrifices to their greedy chieftain and our greedy king. Now we're all paying the price.

After hours pass, I decide I can't do nothing any longer. I have to help those who have been drawn into this horrible mess. It's in my blood. My father was a healer, too, and spent his life trying to minimize pain and restore what was broken.

Gathering up a small pack of medical supplies, I throw the bag over my shoulder and head out. My cat, Arri, watches me go with a forlorn face. People underestimate how much animals understand us, and how many of our feelings they can also feel. I know what I'm doing is dangerous, walking right into the beating heart of battle, but I have nothing to fear except leaving Arri alone.

He would do just fine without me, though. He always has.

My feet crunch along the forest floor as I make my way toward the billowing smoke, and as the miles pass, the scent of burned flesh grows stronger.

That's when my foot collides with something heavy. Not a rock—no, it's softer than that, but not by much. I glance down and find myself face-to-face with an orc.

I jump back, ready to defend myself, but he's out cold. I can tell by the way he's disturbed the ground that he dragged himself a long way, all while absolutely riddled with shrapnel. What are we doing out there? It's inhuman.

Though I shouldn't be getting this close to an orc, I crouch down next to him to get a better look at his wounds. His face is unharmed besides an old scar that runs over his lip, and it isn't a bad face as far as orcs go. He has sturdy brows and high cheekbones. Two small tusks emerge from his mouth, pulling up his lips just slightly at the corners. His ears are pointed but not long like a troll's, and he wears fur-lined leather armor around his bulky, muscled body.

The shrapnel is buried in him all along one side. There are dozens of little pieces of metal sticking out of him at horrific angles, blood dripping from each wound. He will certainly die from blood loss unless I do something. Even then, I wonder, would he survive?

Perhaps my energy would be better spent searching for our own wounded, for humans caught up in this terrible battle. But as I stand up to leave him here, I find I can't take a step.

It wouldn't be right. He probably didn't choose to be here.

It's clear that this orc tried his hardest to leave the war behind and fight for his life. Perhaps there are others back home he wanted to return to, family and friends he cared about, and he dragged himself all the way out here trying to get home to them.

I kneel back down and look over his wounds. His chances of surviving, even if I can patch him up, are slim.

But if my father were here, I know what he'd say: You have to try.

BLIZZEK

Burning. Everything is burning.

My body, the walls of the fortress, my unit scattered around me. It's all on fire, a raging storm of smoke and ash and pain.

But then someone pours water on me. I've been turned over onto my back. I can feel small hands traveling up and down my side, searching out the most searing flames and rubbing something cool and smooth over them. The fire starts to quiet down, hot to the touch but no longer ablaze, like the coals at the bottom of a cooking pit.

That's when the pieces start to come out. Immediately I want to roar and twist and attack whoever is tearing at my flesh, but I can't reach my own body or work my arms and legs. I lie there prone, barely breathing, as white-hot pokers sear through my skin and rip holes into me.

"*Sayan*," a voice croons. "*Ayu sayan.*" It reminds me of my mother's voice, quiet and soothing. I can't understand the words.

We've been fighting humans since before even my grandfather was born. I've heard their language, Freysian, before—and it grates on my bones. But right now, this voice speaking in the human tongue isn't there to hurt me. I know this in a deep place I don't have words to describe.

One by one, every thorn in my side is removed, each one sending a bolt of agony through me fiercer than the previous one. The voice continues to comfort me, assuring me in a tone that says I'll survive whatever is happening, and I try my best to believe it until that last foreign object is finally ripped out.

And then there's more pain. Liquid is being poured into each of my gaping wounds. It's torture to be forced to feel and not react, to simply lie there and absorb every defilement as it's inflicted.

She's still speaking, gently pausing between each wound to clean up and soothe. But it's not over yet. No, it will never be over.

Then comes the pinprick of a needle, lancing through my skin, again and again. It feels as if the torment will never end. Each of the gaping openings is being forced back together and stitched up.

Someone is trying to fix me.

I'm almost near consciousness when the gentle hands finally stop. Some time goes by, and then suddenly, I'm being dragged by one arm and hefted up onto something hard and wooden. That's when everything goes dark again.

CHAPTER 2

NERA

He's in even worse shape than I thought.

I fix up what I can where I found him, because moving a creature of his size would be nearly impossible by myself. I don't have the luxury of getting him on a clean surface with all of my tools spread out around me. I'll just have to do with the dusty forest floor and what I brought along with me in my pack.

I try to ease the pain with salve, and then get to work on cleaning and stitching up the worst of his wounds. But what will I do with him after that?

I could leave him here, I suppose, now that I've done my best to treat him. Due diligence. But then the idea strikes me to bring the wagon with the back gate that folds out. Maybe if I'm really enterprising, I can get him away from the combat zone and tend to his wounds properly.

Back at the house, I retrieve our one horse—whom Refiel

had playfully named Potato—and hook him up to the wagon. I wonder if the orc will have woken and left by the time I get back. I've heard orcs are sturdy.

Strangely, I hope he's still there.

It takes me a while to find him again, but there he is: A huge creature with skin the color of the darkened trees and a head of black hair riddled with small braids, some of them beaded with bone. I had to cut into some of his clothes to get to his wounds, and now he's covered in stitches all over one side of his body, but at least he still has a pulse. It's surprisingly strong given how much blood he's lost.

Potato waits patiently while I open the wagon and then start trying to drag the orc's body up the ramp. He's even bigger than I thought he was. He's hard and dense, like a rock, and I'm only able to move him a few inches at a time by dragging one of his huge arms. I'm going to have to re-clean all of his wounds when I get him back home.

Back home. Am I really going to bring this monster into my house? But where else do I have to put him?

Finally, the orc is most of the way into the wagon and I'm sweating and gasping. Potato is patient as I lead him along at a snail's pace, and the orc is so heavy that he stays right where I put him even as the wagon bumps over rocks and branches.

Then I have to do the same process all over again when we reach the house, even though I've brought the wagon as close to the front door as I can. After making a clean spot for my patient on the floor with a sheepskin to go under his body, I return to drag him inside. I have to take a break partway through, but eventually, I get him settled and then go to put Potato away.

The orc is breathing deeper now as if perhaps he's fallen asleep. I gently clean off his wounds and decide to let him stay like that. It will help in the healing process if he can get some genuine rest.

I sit down at the table and rest my head in my hands. After staying up all night listening to the war going on outside and then bringing this creature home with me, I'm exhausted, too. I pledge to stay awake and watch over him, just in case he starts to fever, but before long my eyelids are drifting closed, and the orc's gentle breathing lulls me into a dreamless sleep.

Blizzek

When I wake up, the first thing I notice is the smell. It's floral and fresh, like herbs and flowers.

My eyes are crusted when I open them. I try to lift my hands to rub my face, but only one of my arms will move properly. When I look down at the disobedient arm, I find puckered, stitched wounds running down my bicep, my chest, and my side. Just tilting my head sends a shock of agony down my spine.

All right, don't move. Not yet, anyway.

I take in the rest of my surroundings. I'm in a house, clearly of human design, with crisscrossing wooden beams in the ceiling and bare wood walls. I'm on the floor near a small fireplace, which still has some smoldering logs in it. I hear quiet breaths in and out.

There's someone here with me. I'm in danger.

As much as it hurts, I crane my neck around to look. There's no way I can get up and run in this state. But when I see her hunched over a table, head laying her in crossed arms, I don't think that will be a problem—for now.

A human woman sits there, fast asleep. A braid of long,

dark hair hangs over her shoulder. Her skin is bronze and gleaming, but most of it is hidden by civilian clothing. She's clearly no soldier. All the skin that I can see is soft and smooth and without blemish.

How have I ended up here? It must be some sort of elaborate trap.

That smell. It's drawing me over to the pile of herbs and medicines scattered around the sheepskin rug where I've been placed, along with a mortar and pestle, jars full of salve, and bundles of dry leaves.

A healer. She found me and brought me back here, inside her own home.

I wonder if she's alone. Has she told the other humans? This could be the precursor to becoming a prisoner, the worst fate to befall any trollkin. Rotting away in a cell, used as a bargaining chip, kept like a destitute pet. I would rather die.

I try once again to get up, but the entire left side of my body is fighting me. I groan and fall back to lying flat on the rug.

"Mm?" The woman raises her head, her eyes fluttering open. They're big and brown—a rich, full color, like warm earth. When she sees me looking back at her, I expect her to scream. But all she does is smile gently at me. "Ah. *Aya raan.*"

NERA

"Ah, you're awake." The only thing I feel when I see the orc looking back at me is relief. He made it. That was his first big hurdle. I have much more hope now that he'll recover.

But his face is anything but relieved. He's angry—no, furious. His eyes are as hard as stones and his teeth are grit together, and I wonder if I've made a grievous error in bringing him here.

I didn't consider that he might choose to kill me.

The orc tries to move, perhaps to attack, but he groans as his wounds hold him back. He falls down to the rug once more, shivering in pain. Without thinking about what I'm doing, I get out of my chair and kneel down next to him, retrieving my calming remedy once more.

"Let me apply some of this," I say, "and it will help with the pain."

The orc simply snarls at me when I try to get close. Maybe he can't get up in his current state, but he can fight me off. It was much easier to deal with him when he was unconscious.

"I'm trying to help." I hold up the jar. "See? You can smell it." I bring it under my nose and inhale to show him what I mean.

The orc growls at me again, but I take a glop of salve and bring my hand down to the wound on his arm. He tries to move it away, but he only causes himself even more pain. If he keeps flailing like this, his wounds will open again and I'll have to stitch him back up. Fat chance he'll let me get a second try.

Using my other hand, I pin his arm down and start rubbing his wound with the balm. He lets out an enraged roar and reaches for me with his good arm... then he feels the coolness of the remedy working on him, and he stops. His mouth relaxes as the soothing compounds seep in, cooling the hot, angry skin. It won't do much to relieve the internal pain, but it will numb the area significantly, and hopefully reduce his irritation a little.

Slowly his arm drops to his side as I continue to rub the salve around the wounds. There's still fury and resentment on his face as I work, and he doesn't take his eyes off me for a moment. They're a strangely bright amber, like a sky at sunset.

He says something to me in Trollkin in his guttural voice, but I can't understand it. I shake my head.

"I'm sorry," I say. "I don't understand." I continue down his side, pushing away his torn clothes as much as I can to get to each of his injuries. His muscle is dense everywhere I touch. I've never seen such brute strength packed into one place. When I reach his hip and pull aside his coil, I hear another snarl of warning. My hands are rather close to the place between his legs. He is understandably protective of it.

"Don't worry." I try to use my most calming voice. I need him to trust me if I'm going to do this. I hold up my hands to show my intentions: I'm only going to touch what I need to treat him.

He continues to snarl but does not move to act as I trace the wound on his groin muscle. I continue on to his thigh, which is as thick as a tree trunk.

Out of the corner of my eye, I see a lump starting to grow underneath his leather pants, or what remains of them. When I glance up at his face, the orc is now carefully looking away from me.

How can he manage to get one of those now, when his blood is already in such short supply? It must be a good sign if he feels that well. Maybe it's an instinctual reaction. I won't assume it has anything to do with me.

After making my way down his leg with my treatment, I scoot back and look at my handiwork. There's still blood oozing from most of the big wounds, but it's started to cake up and harden. That's good—his body is trying to protect itself. Hopefully, the balm has eased at least some of his pain.

Not only has the lump between his legs not gone away, it's grown even bigger. I catch the orc staring at me, but when I try to return his look, he turns away again.

I should be horrified by this, deep down. But I find that I'm not.

No, instead I'm wondering what he thinks of me. Am I doing this to him, or is it a memory of someone else? Or perhaps a response to the shock he simply can't control?

I get up off the floor and decide it's time to get to work. He needs some food and fluids in him if he's going to get through this.

CHAPTER 3

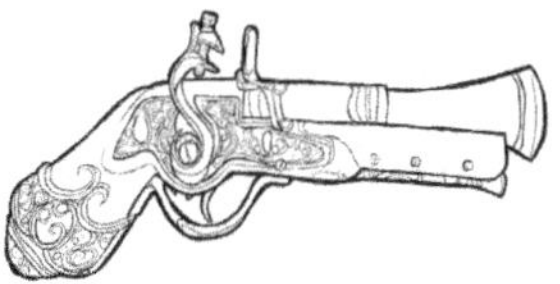

BLIZZEK

Absolutely humiliating. As embarrassing as it gets, really.

I'm getting a raging hard-on—for a human.

As much as I threaten her, and make it clear I'll rip her skin off her bones if she touches me, the woman with the braid and the soft, rounded cheeks doesn't back off. She won't, I can see it in her eyes. And so I give in. What else can I do when I can't even move?

Besides, the cool salve on my skin is a relief. I can still feel the bone-deep pain, but on the surface, it has started to numb me, and the pain lessens right away. So I decide to let her continue what she's doing if she's so intent.

Strangest of all is how good she looks doing it. She probably has no idea how her shirt falls open as she crouches over me, applying one dab of salve after another. Almost all of her chest is exposed under the collar: A bounty of smooth, copper skin in two perfect mounds, barely held in. I can't help the immediate reaction my body has to her.

I've never found a human attractive. They are small and fragile and vile. Their kind has dropped bombs of shrapnel on top of us, tearing our bodies apart. I should hate her with the very fiber of my being.

But she continues her ministrations with the soft hands of someone who certainly doesn't hate me, and I don't know what to make of her. Why is a human taking care of me at all? She could have just left me out there where she found me, but instead she decided to treat me. Somehow, alone, she brought me all the way back here to what I can only assume is her home, and now she's doing everything in her power to make sure I'm comfortable.

I really have no idea what to make of it. None at all.

When she's finished applying her medicine, she stands up and walks away to what looks like her kitchen. Her legs are long, and she wears a skirt to cover them that falls just below her knees. From my angle, I can see most of her thigh, which is supple but not weak. Without intending to, I imagine what's just out of sight, above that thigh. I can make out the curve of her hip under her clothes, and it's delicious.

I curse at myself. Mostly, at my dick. How could it betray me like this?

She's gone for a while, and I use the opportunity to close my eyes and take deep, calming breaths. Slowly my cock starts to relax, and I use all the orc will I've built up in my life to keep it that way when she returns to the room, carrying a tray full of food.

I don't realize how hungry I am until the smell hits me. On the tray, I can make out some dried meat, fruit, bread, and cheese. When she sets it down next to me, all I want is to pick it up and dump it into my mouth whole.

But when I try to sit up, I'm hit with the same miserable pain as before. I can't even lift my neck enough to reach anything.

The human says something in Freysian I can't understand and gently presses down on my good shoulder to show me I should stay put. I don't know why, but I listen right away and stop moving. With a nod of approval, she picks up some bread, slathering it in butter before bringing it to my lips.

Wait. There's no way she's about to feed me.

She says something that I'm almost positive means *open up*. Her voice is like smooth, golden honey, and the smell of the butter is so intoxicating that I obey without meaning to.

It tastes like heaven. Before I realize it, I'm chewing frantically, then swallowing and taking another bite. I can't think of a deeper humiliation than letting a human hand-feed me because I'm too weak to eat on my own, but I can't seem to stop. She feeds me a piece of fruit next, and the juices stream down the sides of my mouth. Without blinking, she reaches across and dabs it up with her skirt, then offers me another piece.

Something in my chest is twisting, tightening, squeezing so hard I almost can't breathe. The tenderness on her face as she feeds me some cheese on bread is like a slice of shrapnel. How can she possibly look at me that way? It doesn't make any sense.

I close my eyes as I swallow the rest of the food because I can't bear to look at her and see my pathetic face reflected in her eyes.

I shouldn't be alive, and yet I'm still here because of some miserable human.

NERA

This time, the orc barely fights me at all. Partway through my feeding him, he closes his eyes, and there's a fresh look of pain on his face.

No, it's embarrassment. His pride has just taken a massive blow by allowing me to feed him. This is a creature with an ego the size of a mountain, and here he is, climbing down it so a human can help him live.

"I'm sorry," I say to him once the food is finished. His eyes are still closed, as if he can't stand to look at me. "It must be painful for you."

He doesn't say anything. I know he can't understand me anyway, but I hope that at least some of my tone gets across.

I give him some water, but not too much, and then leave the room to let him rest in peace.

In the meantime, I busy myself in the garden. It's late in the day to be doing my chores, but my morning was a little occupied. I water and pull weeds, wiping my hands on my skirt as I go. It's always been a bad habit of mine that Refiel tried to break. "It takes twice as long to wash the clothes when you do that," he always said, but it's just convenient.

I wonder what he would think of me bringing an injured orc back to our home, right in the middle of a war. Would he approve? I can't say that I know the answer, and that makes me sadder than anything. I'm starting to forget him already.

When I return with a basket full of radishes, greens, and a little corn, I peek into the other room to check on the orc I brought home. He lies on his back with his eyes closed, but his breathing isn't so deep and even as to indicate sleep.

After cleaning the produce, I check his wounds again. I just use my eyes this time, and while the cuts and gashes are all red, none of them look too angry. No infection yet.

The orc opens his eyes as I kneel there, and slowly turns them on me. Those strange, amber irises are full of emotion. Confusion, regret, anger, humiliation. He doesn't understand why I've brought him here. He hates that he's helpless. There's nothing I can do to make him feel any better about that except to treat him and hope he makes it, so he can be right once again.

When he can finally move, I wonder, will I be safe? Will he take this second chance and use it to exact his revenge on humankind through me? I hadn't considered it when I brought him here because he was so helpless, but that won't always be the case.

I take a breath and focus on the now. I have no idea what he'll do in the future. I have one job, and that's to nurse him back to health just like Father would have. So I return the orc's stare and try to funnel everything I can into that one look.

Safety. Calm. Trust. Perhaps if I can earn his trust, he won't kill me or burn my house down, as I know orcs are wont to do.

He looks surprised at what he receives and quickly turns his head away again. His mouth settles into a deep frown, so I rise to my feet and leave him alone.

I finish my chores as the sun starts to set and wonder what the night will bring.

BLIZZEK

That look on the human woman's face was the very last thing I expected to see reflected back at me. Her eyes were like huge pools that I wanted nothing more than to step into and sink in their warm waters.

I jerk myself out of it. Maybe this human has some kind of

magic that goes with her healer abilities. Something about her makes me feel calm in a way I never have before, and I wonder if she has me hypnotized.

The woman returns to her work in the other room, and I try to get some sleep. That's the best thing I can do for myself right now—sleep and regain my strength so I can leave here. There's no way I'll stay here for an hour longer than I need to.

I'll leave her alive, though, after everything she's done for me. As much as I hate humankind, this one woman decided to break ranks and help me, despite the fact I could end her with my bare hands. I've killed more of her countrymen than I can possibly count, and yet she took me in.

It's difficult not to think of Raz'jin and his wild human female. Humans are clearly capable of being tantalizing creatures. Maybe he was hypnotized this way, too, and look where that got him. He's probably dead out there along with everyone else we came into this war with.

But I can't shake the feeling that this woman is different. Even as the conflict rages around her she remains at her small house, caring for me. The air around her is so peaceful, so quiet and nurturing that it feels like she's created an impenetrable bubble around us.

I sleep until the sun has set, and when I wake up, the woman sits at the table once again with a candle burning in front of her. She's writing something on a sheaf of paper, focused intently on her work. She hasn't noticed I'm awake yet, so I simply watch her. Her brow is furrowed in concentration as she writes, and she hunches over a little farther than she probably should, like she's passionate about whatever words she's scribbling down onto the page. She's wearing warmer clothes now, and I'm grateful because all it would take is a glimpse of one of her round breasts to make me—

Damn it. I exhale and breathe evenly to relax my impossible cock. On top of the pain that lances through my muscles whenever I even flex my lungs, I do not need this. But the sound must have caught her attention, because the human woman looks over at me, and she smiles when she sees that I'm awake.

That smile is like a warm fire on a cold winter night. There's a candymaker in Kalishagg who produces caramel-covered apples, and her smile reminds me of biting into one, the hot-and-cold sweetness filling my mouth.

She says a pleasant-sounding greeting in Freysian, then sits beside me again, holding out a cup of water. Even though it hurts like a bitch, I reach for it with my good hand, and I bring my head up just far enough to drink.

"*Suma,*" she says, nodding in approval like I've just passed a test. There's a glimmer of hope in her eyes. She's worried, I realize at that moment, that I won't live through this.

Little does she know that orcs are resilient. While everything crashes and burns around us, we will persist.

She takes the cup back from me but doesn't move away again. The human woman is just studying me, taking in the sight of my face, my chest. And then she registers my crotch, where my infernal dick has started making itself known again. But she doesn't look the least bit offended. Certainly not embarrassed. She just smiles again, as if I've paid her a great compliment.

She holds her hand to her chest. "Nera," she says.

Another Freysian word I don't understand. I roll my eyes with impatience. I'm not going to learn their miserable human language.

Her expression falls a little. But she tries again, more urgently this time. She points at herself and says, "*Eyn* Nera."

I think she's trying to introduce herself. Something about

that strikes me as funny, as if we've just met for the first time in a bar.

"Blizzek," I answer. There's no harm in it, is there? "I'm Blizzek."

There's a warm look on her face as she absorbs this, and then repeats it back to me. "Blizzek." She makes a face like the name tastes good.

"Nera," I say, pointing at her. It's a pretty name as far as human names go, and simple to wrap my mouth around.

And at this, the human woman *blushes*.

CHAPTER 4

I don't know what it is about the way he says my name, combined with the stiff hard-on between his legs, that makes me suddenly feel a rush of embarrassment. No, it's not that—it's something else I can't quite put my finger on.

Pleasure.

That's what it is. This is the second time he's had this reaction, and it's made a burst of heat rush from my chest into my face, and then down again to the little cavern between my legs.

I can't believe I'm thinking this way. Not only is he my patient, but he's an orc. A creature. A trollkin. His people and mine have fought for longer than we've both been alive—as long as our two peoples have existed, most likely.

And yet knowing that something about my presence is turning him on makes me feel alive in a way I haven't felt since Refiel was still here.

All I have to do is think of his name and immediately, I feel guilty. It's only been a year and a half since my husband was pulled into the war, and a few months after that, I got word that he had been killed in battle. Certainly by a trollkin. Perhaps even an orc, just like the one lying in front of me.

I quickly get up and retreat to the other room, where I can take a few deep, calming breaths. Maybe his hard-on is just an instinctual reaction to his injuries. I'm taking it far too seriously.

I don't return again except to put out the candle and pick up my notes. I was writing a letter to Refiel about everything that's happened, in the hope that I could glean some wisdom from it. The orc's—Blizzek's—eyes are closed now, but I can tell he's not asleep.

"Goodnight," I say to him, then walk into my bedroom. There, I try to fall asleep for an hour, maybe two, but all I can think about is the orc on my sheepskin rug. His big, square jaw; the shocking amber of his eyes; the smooth curve of his groin muscle from his hip inward to a place I can't even bring myself to imagine.

I miss Refiel in more ways than one, and pleasures of the body are certainly on the list. I try to remember him as I slide my hand down between my legs, but when I start to touch my soft folds, the face I keep seeing is the one lying right outside my room. I run my fingers across my clit, over and over, as everything starts to grow warm and swollen. Then I duck one inside my slick entrance, and I can't help a little gasp. I rub my juices all over myself, then speed up.

Unbidden, an image of Blizzek sitting upright, crouched over me, springs into my mind. He pulls down his leather pants and underneath... I let out a tiny moan when I picture it. It's not difficult to summon after seeing what I saw earlier. He's large, I know that. I wonder what he would feel like. It's been so long since someone—something—filled me up as much as I need, and I know that he would more than fill me.

I can't believe I'm here, thinking about this, imagining what his orc cock might look like. But I can't stop now. I'm almost there. I rub myself even faster, my breaths coming out short and fast. Then I put two fingers inside myself, and that's almost enough to give me the fullness I'm craving. He would be much bigger than this, of course. And he would be able to go deep, deep into that empty place that waits with longing.

Finally, the little explosion of pleasure hits me right in the throat, and I shudder as my climax travels all the way through to my toes. It was nothing spectacular, but I feel a little better as my release floods my bloodstream.

It's easier to fall asleep after that. But when I dream, I dream of fire and screaming. Instead of being inside my house, I'm there, in the middle of the fight. I'm looking down as bits of shrapnel wedge themselves into my skin, and everything burns.

Blizzek

Does she not think I can hear her?

Perhaps her weak human ears really believe that she's being quiet. But oh, no, I can hear every last one of her labored breaths.

She's really going at it, too. Her gasps quicken, and within seconds I'm as hard as timber. This is a little less shocking. Overhearing a woman's moans of pleasure is a perfectly understandable reason for getting a raging boner.

But as she continues in the next room, clearly growing closer to her breaking point, I try to reach down so I can deal with my little problem—and find that I can't. No, my body screams when I try to move, and not even my good arm can reach far enough to push down my pants and take my cock in my hand.

Damn it. Damn it to hell. I have to just sit there and listen, my body and my dick aching in very different ways, while she brings herself to the top of the peak. I think of those two perfect breasts as she crouched over me, and what she might look like underneath that skirt. I imagine her fingers on herself, and try to picture her little pinkish-brown cunt. It's probably shiny and small, much too small for someone like me to fit inside, certainly.

As she finally crests in the other room, I wish more than anything else I could simply pump one out, but instead I'm now lying here with a huge boner between my legs that I can't do anything about.

After a time her breaths even out, and I'm certain that she's asleep. I wonder what that soft, round face looks like as she sleeps. I imagine her pouty lips letting out tiny breaths, her long eyelashes spread across her cheeks.

This is really only making it worse, but I can't stop. My balls are tight and ready to unload, and there's nothing I can do about it.

Eventually, I do manage to drift off. Instead of dreaming of war, I dream of getting off the floor and walking into the little human's bedroom. I dream of climbing onto her bed on top of her as she wakes up and finds me there. She lets out a little shout of surprise, which I quickly silence with a kiss. Soon she stops fighting, and as I bring her up into my arms, she lets me. I lift her skirt around her hips and her lower lips are already wet and swollen up with desire.

It's so easy to slide myself in that I have to restrain myself from coming right away. No, I'm going to hold on. I'm going to get her so lathered up for me that it's like fucking in a bath. Once she's moaning underneath me and dragging her nails across my chest, that's when I let her have it. I pump and thrust as hard as I can until she's crying out my name, and then I sink my cock deep inside her.

No, wait. I want my dream self to pull out, to eject all over her belly, but he won't do it. He groans as he fills her up, and collapses on top of her.

It can't be me doing such an unspeakable thing as fucking a human woman, right?

NERA

Even though I had so much trouble falling asleep, I'm up as soon as the sun is. It's time to check on the orc and then take care of the sheep.

He's sleeping soundly when I enter the main room. I squat near him to take a look at his wounds, and I'm impressed with what I find. They're already starting to heal underneath my stitches. I've never seen anything like it.

Orcs truly are resilient creatures. He might just make it out of this.

After I let out the sheep, I start working on breakfast. I have a few eggs still that I traded some produce for before all of this happened, but I'm running low. Unfortunately, Blizzek will need plenty of protein if he's going to heal properly, so I not only fill the plate with eggs but also cheese and more meat. I might have to slaughter a sheep if this keeps up.

By the time I return to his side, the orc is awake. His neck is able to move more when I sit down to feed him, and this time, he can move his other arm enough to take the food away from me. It's a dramatic improvement over yesterday. I leave him to his devices as he eats ravenously, and I'm immensely pleased to see he has an appetite.

It won't be long though until he has to use certain other bodily functions, and I'm not sure how I'm going to be able to move him enough for that. In the meantime, I bring in a chamber pot and set it near him. Instantly he recognizes what it is, and another snarl pinches his lips.

"You're going to have to do it eventually," I say, even though I know he can't understand me. I use a stern but gentle voice, nodding at the chamber pot, and he snarls again. But we both know he'll need it, so I leave it where it is and take the empty tray of food away.

"*Gak agnek*," he says. Naturally, I don't understand Trollkin, but when I look up at his face, I have a good idea of what it means. For once his scowl isn't quite as deep. I think maybe he's thanking me.

I have to smile at that. I dip my head slightly as I say, "You're welcome." He seems to understand this and returns to his position lying flat.

The rest of the day passes much like this. I go out to do chores and find Arri has secured himself a mouse for a meal. I watch him tear out the guts for a few minutes before returning to check on Blizzek again.

He watches me as I move about the house, and there doesn't seem to be any more shame or embarrassment about it. It must be terribly boring to lie there all day, so that evening, I sit down on the floor by him and bring out one of my favorite games. It involves flipping over clay tokens and making sets of patterns, and taking away the tokens whenever you make a match between three or more. The player with the most tokens at the end wins.

It takes a while to show him how it works, and at first,

Blizzek isn't interested at all. But he needs to do something with his mind if he's going to heal, so I insist on demonstrating the rules again. Eventually, he lets out a sigh of irritation and gently rolls onto his side so that he can see better. I'm impressed that he can even move that much.

We play a few rounds, and after the first game, he starts to beat me handily. He has a quick mind—that much I can tell. I always thought trollkin were rather simple beasts, but that isn't so for my orc.

My orc. The words cross my mind before I can think twice about them.

After my fifth loss in a row, I toss all the tokens back in the box with a little more annoyance than I intended. That's when Blizzek laughs. He says something in Trollkin I can't understand, but by his tone, I can tell the meaning: *Sore loser.*

"So what?" I ask, huffing as I get to my feet. It was my game, after all. But he just laughs again and rolls onto his back once more.

This time, when I apply the salve to his wounds, Blizzek is much more obedient and pliable. He's less so when I clean them, though, and hisses as the solution burns his wounds.

"I'm sorry," I say. Nodding in understanding, he responds with something in Trollkin. I wonder if this means, *It's all right.*

When I have to fix one of the stitches, and he starts to snarl again, I repeat the words back to him. *"It's all right."*

His eyes open wide at this. He's shocked that I've used his own language to communicate with him. That isn't so outrageous, is it? But there's a surprising softness in those amber irises, like it touched him that I even bothered to try.

Not only is my orc smart, but he has a deep well of emotions, too—I can see it inside him. He just happens to use some emotions more than others.

When I retreat to my room that night, my mind isn't shy

about showing me what I want. It's Blizzek's warm eyes, his sharply defined muscles, the big lump hiding under his pants. I'm just lonely, I tell myself, as I imagine taking off those pants and finding out what he really looks like. As I imagine him rubbing that big cock against me, then sliding into me. I orgasm easily and wonder what's becoming of me.

CHAPTER 5

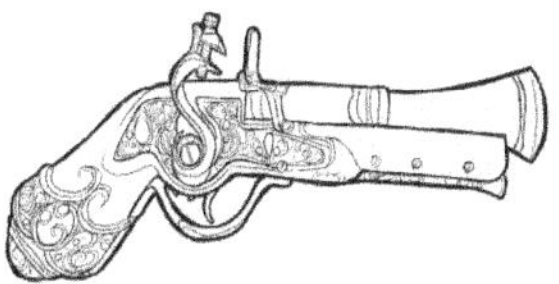

BLIZZEK

I think this woman is hell-bent on torturing me.

I hear her going at it again, and my dick responds immediately. Traitorous bastard. And I'm still too immobile to do anything about it. All I can really do is fantasize—and boy, do I ever. I try to think about orcesses I've fucked in the past, the many trollkin women I've picked up at bars and then taken back to my room, and what it felt like to plunder each one of them.

But whenever I try to picture one, I see little Nera instead. And I can't seem to do anything about it.

I lie awake, wondering what I'm going to do once I finally get out of here. If I can make it back to camp unharmed—given that camp is still even there—I'll be sent out onto the front lines again, just another body to add to the pile. But I can't go back to Kalishagg, not without earning the mark of a deserter and facing death.

I keep expecting the trollkin forces to arrive at any

moment, breaking down the door and killing the little human woman who's been dutifully nursing me back to health. Surely they'll discover this place sooner or later.

But when I picture this, something inside me aches. Maybe I should stay, and make sure that if this happens, they don't get a chance to write home about it.

No. As soon as I get the chance, I'm leaving.

The next day, Nera is impressed at how rapidly I'm healing, admiring my wounds vocally. She brings me food again, and again I'm able to eat on my own. She looks like a proud parent.

"Thank you," she says to me in Trollkin. Again, I'm shocked she's remembered it, not to mention bothered to use it. And why is she thanking me, anyway? She's the one who brought me food.

"You're welcome," I respond anyway. She mimics me, then nods as she learns the word. She seems intent on communicating with me when there's really no need for that. We have nothing to talk about.

Nera apparently has much do around the house, so whenever she's out, I take the opportunity to sleep. The more I can sleep, the faster my body will work to repair itself, I know this much. I've endured many great wounds simply by finding a hole to sleep in until I've strengthened enough to get to a healer.

It isn't long before my smaller wounds have already closed up. Nera takes my arm in her lap and marvels at me. I don't pull it back. She says a few words in Freysian, tracing my puckered skin with her finger, and it sends shivers running up into my chest. What is she doing to me? Now any small touch brings my infernal crotch to life. But Nera doesn't seem to mind, and it certainly doesn't deter her from continuing on with her little wellness check.

That night, when she brings out the game with the clay

tokens, I assume she's forgiven me for kicking her ass the last time. Now I'm even able to sit up some, and at first, Nera tries to stop me, as if I'll rip open all my stitches. But I wave her off. "I'm fine."

She arches an eyebrow, then sighs and shakes her head. I'm a rather difficult patient, I imagine.

This time when we play, she keeps up with me a little better. The way her mouth tilts down and her brows furrow together when I make a good play is adorable, so I keep making them.

It's disgusting, if I'm being honest, to find her attractive—and yet I also can't stop.

Every night her moans start up again, and they haunt me. I wish I could tell her to please, just stop it. I know if I asked, she would. But how? I'm overcome with humiliation just thinking about how I would convey that to her.

Besides, this is her own home. She can do what she wants. I'm a guest here, and I'm going to be gone before I overstay my welcome.

NERA

Blizzek is improving at such a rapid rate that it won't be long before he can properly move again. It might be longer before he can actually walk—some of his primary thigh and calf muscles took big hits, and they will take time to knit back together properly—but I have no illusions about what will happen once he can.

No, I don't think he'll burn my house down. But he'll certainly return to where he came from, and that will be the end of it.

The first day he's able to sit up on his own to eat, I cheer. It startles him, and he almost drops his food.

"I'm sorry," I say in Trollkin. This was an easy one to learn. He always gets that surprised look on his face when I speak to him in his own tongue, and I worry that I've insulted him by trying. But then he smiles and tells me that it's all right, and I think I might be improving.

Blizzek doesn't sleep nearly as much that day, so when I'm done with my chores I sit on the floor with him to play the token game. But he doesn't seem very interested in it today.

"Sugnak, grren," he says. I have no idea what the words mean, or what he's trying to convey with them. He indicates to the table, where my ink and quill sit with the paper I write my letters on.

"Oh. You want to write something?" I bring the ink and quill to the floor where he can reach them. He starts to draw on the paper, and what I expected to be rudimentary pictures are actually quite lovely. He draws objects and starts putting words to them. I learn things like *woman* and *man* (with quite funny images to go along with them), as well as *human* and *trollkin*. While Arri spent the first few days hiding out after I brought Blizzek home, now he shows himself more often. Blizzek teaches me the Trollkin word for *cat*, and Arri seems to like it well enough that he rubs himself up against the orc's side. Blizzek tentatively pets the cat on the head, and I have to smile. He has a gentleness to him that wasn't obvious at first, and it tickles me low in my belly. Just how gentle is he?

Whenever my thoughts go to this place—which they do, obnoxiously often—I try to remember Refiel. My husband. The man I'd thought I was going to spend my entire life with. What would he think of what I'm doing now?

Blizzek must see a strange look come over my face because he halts the drawing he's been making. It's a rather detailed one. Beautiful, honestly. He's talented and seems to have no idea.

"*Are you all right?*" he asks, and I can actually understand the words even if they seem to slur together.

It's such a kind and considerate thing that fondness swells in my chest.

"*Yes,*" I say. I wish I could communicate that I'm just momentarily sad and it will pass, but I don't know how. But the more I think about Refiel, and all the parts of our life together that have started to fall away from my memory, the more my heart twists inside my chest.

Blizzek studies me as these emotions cross my face. He leans down and draws a pair of eyes with tears coming out, and repeats a word a few times. I think it means *sad*, so I repeat it back to him.

"*Are you sad?*" he asks.

And I have to nod, because why lie? I have nothing to hide from Blizzek. We are essentially strangers.

"*Why?*"

I know this word now, too, but I don't have a way to answer it. So instead I get up and go to find the one thing that might explain the idea of Refiel.

I return with a painting that was done for us as a wedding gift. It's not the best depiction, but anyone could tell from looking at it that it's us. I lean it up against the table and gesture at the image.

At first, Blizzek looks quite perplexed by this new introduction.

"*Why are you sad?*" he asks again.

I cover Refiel's face with my hand, so it's just me, alone in the painting.

In that moment, I can tell that Blizzek understands. His

expression falters, and when he looks at me with those sharp amber eyes, I can see sympathy in them.

"I'm sorry," he says. I just nod, and then put the painting away again. But seeing Refiel's face has refilled a well of misery that I thought I had already emptied. I call our token game early that night and put it away before Blizzek is done making his final move. But he doesn't object—he just watches me as I busy around, getting ready for bed.

"Goodnight," I say to him in Trollkin.

"Goodnight, Nera."

I think it's the first time that he's used my name. I just smile and nod, trying to keep the tears building behind my eyes packed away. But once I'm alone in my room again, they come rolling out in great, terrible waves. I try to keep it as quiet as I can.

BLIZZEK

Who was he? Her mate?

Humans don't have this concept, but I imagine it's something similar to that. It clearly brought her an immense amount of pain to show me the painting, because I heard her crying in her bedroom not long after.

So she's lost someone to all of this, too. This war has stolen someone she loved, and still, she took me in. She cared for me, even when I pushed her away. She's fed me and ensured my comfort.

I wonder what I did in a past life to deserve this.

At least now I can control my damned boners around her, and at night when she goes to bed, I can reach far enough to get my cock out. It's painful to do, but I do it anyway because late at night she's all I can think about. I imagine the gentle curve of her hip under her skirts, the swell of her breasts without her shirt to keep her inside, and her huge, deep brown eyes. I wonder what those eyes would look like as I slid my cock inside her. What does her mouth do when she's being pleasured? I've heard her soft moans before, and all I have to do is overlay them on the play happening in my mind to come all over myself.

Great. Once I've done it, I realize I hadn't considered how to clean up afterward. I rub it off on my clothes, which are already filthy by now, and try to go to sleep.

It's as if she can read my mind, because the next day, Nera enters the room carrying a small armful of clothing. At first, I don't understand what she's thinking because none of it has any chance of fitting me. But instead, she starts to cut each piece up, then fits them to my body, and starts sewing them back together by hand. I wonder if the stench of my sweat, blood, and come-covered clothes has finally reached the breaking point.

"Please?" she asks, reaching for the bottom of my jerkin. I can sit up now without blinding pain, so I nod my head. Instead of pulling it off of me, she cuts it off. She clearly has no interest in trying to save it. Soon I'm topless in the middle of her living room.

Nera's eyes traverse me from collar to groin and back again, her mouth slightly ajar. Only then does she realize what she's done, and her face flushes a bright red. So she likes what she sees, does she? This brings me an immense amount of pleasure. In fact, a little too much pleasure, because soon I'm starting to harden again underneath my pants.

I can tell that Nera notices, but she's pretending not to as she holds the shirt over my head and starts trying to slip it on me. But the wounds in my side and arm are still too fresh, and I can't lift the arm as high as I would need to fit into it.

"I'm sorry," she says, and I'm not sure what she's apologizing for her.

"It's all right."

I lie back down, now committed to the shirtless look until we can get something else on me. I don't even try to hide how she's making me feel because what's the point? An orc has needs. Maybe she'll take the hint and leave the room so I can whack one out.

But that's not what Nera does, not at all. She looks down, right at the lump in my pants, and gets that furrowed look on her face.

"Why?" she asks. It's possibly the sweetest and most humiliating thing she could ask. But her grasp of Trollkin is barely at toddler level, and she doesn't have any other words for it.

Why, indeed? Because she looked at me with a little tinge of desire on her face?

I decide to lie a little and gesture at my bare chest as if my being exposed is a sufficient answer. Quickly Nera nods, and she disappears into her room to find something. She returns with a blanket and puts it over me.

It's such a tender action that something very frightening happens. My chest constricts, and I feel a surge of affection deep in my gut. Then, as if to really seal in the shame, my idiotic cock jumps to full attention.

I can't lie anymore now.

"You," I say. She knows this word now.

"You?" she repeats. Then she corrects herself. "Me?"

Like there's anyone else in the room. I roll my eyes, then look at the cat. "No, I meant him."

I can see her wheels turning, and then, she laughs. It's such a bright sound, like a little bell chime.

Nera nods in understanding. She doesn't seem disgusted like I expected. Surely a kind human woman like her wouldn't want anything to do with me after confessing that she's the reason I can't seem to control my dick.

"Are you all right?" she asks, and it's not in a *How are your wounds?* tone of voice. "Help?"

"Help?" I repeat. "Help me?"

She gestures at herself, and then at me. It's like the world stops turning for a moment.

"With this?" Like an absolute idiot, I gesture at my cock. It's lifting my torn pants right off my hips.

She nods.

I think I might pass out.

Chapter 6

He has no idea what to make of my question.

I understand. I have needs, too. But I'm physically capable of taking care of them.

He's my patient. That's all it is. This is the story I'm telling myself, anyway, even though it's because I want to know what's under there—if it's anything like what I've seen in my imagination.

Quickly Blizzek's surprise is replaced by an emotion I can only describe as anger. He covers his crotch with his good hand and hastily looks away from me.

I've deeply offended him, I realize. Why did I think that would fly?

"I'm sorry," I say, and quickly get up to put the quill and ink away. I'm a complete idiot. How rude and condescending to even suggest it. It was selfish of me.

But before I can take a step, I feel a hand on my ankle. When I look down, Blizzek is halfway sitting up, stopping me from walking away.

"*It's all right.*" He takes a few deep breaths like he's trying to still some creature inside himself. He pulls on me, so I return to a kneeling position again. His hand doesn't leave me and instead comes to rest on my hip.

"*If you want,*" he says carefully. I don't recognize the grammar he's using, so I give him a perplexed look. "*Want?*" he asks again. "*Does Nera want to do this?*"

Oh. So he only wants me to do it if I want to. Not as his healer, but as me, Nera.

Do I? Have I not been imagining him the last few nights and wondering what he would look like, feel like, taste like?

I want to, more than anything. So I nod my head. "*Yes, I want.*"

For a second, Blizzek stops breathing. I can feel that he's itching to get closer, but his stitches won't let him, so he lies leaning back on one elbow. Instead, he says, "*Please.*"

Something about that last word, while he's begging me with his eyes to touch him, starts to heat up a little reservoir inside me. I reach for the knife and gently run it down the other side of his pants, along his good leg. I make sure to go slowly, and as I do, I take in the shape of his muscular legs, the swell of his calf, the strong feet. He has four toes to my five.

Then I pull the fabric away and there he is. His penis is the same color as he is, but a little darker. It's certainly bigger than any other I've seen in my life, almost as long as my forearm—especially as swollen up and thick as it is with blood. It looks just like I'd hoped. No, it's even better, even more enthralling.

Blizzek's breathing is already coming harder and faster than before, and I haven't even touched him yet. I'm worried that he'll change his mind, so I keep my eyes on his while I lower my hands to the monstrous cock in front of me.

It's exactly as soft as I expected. There's a dribble already leaking out the tip, and I spread it around the head with my thumb. This elicits a very sharp gasp. His eyes are focused intently on mine now as I start to move my hand, up and down, keeping my pace slow. He groans and his eyelids close, and his head drifts back onto the floor.

But I want more. Just touching him isn't enough. Suddenly, I want to give him the time of his life.

When I touch my lips to his cock, Blizzek's eyes shoot open, and he looks down at me with surprise. I bring my mouth down the head and then back up again, leaving my hands on his shaft where they were before. This time, I earn a heavy moan. That's what I wanted—to make him feel this way.

His hand travels from where it rests on my hip, around behind me. He squeezes my ass firmly as I continue my way downward. Soon I have as much of him in my mouth as I can fit, and then I start moving my hand and mouth in sync.

His hand clenches me even tighter, and his breath is coming hard and fast now. He just says the word, "Nera," and then suddenly he's swelling up in my hand, his sac tightening against him. When he shoots into my mouth it's far more than I expected, and a whole bunch of it drips down my chin in a very unladylike fashion. I pull up the edge of my skirt and use it to wipe my face.

At this, Blizzek laughs. It's a big belly laugh, after which he recoils and hisses at the immediate pain it probably sent through his injuries.

I tilt my head at him. "*Why?*"

Still breathing hard, Blizzek props himself up on his elbows again and reaches out for my skirt. For a second, I think he's going to pull it right up, but instead, he points to one of the many stains on it—dirt, for the most part, then some grass and his come, too. He just shakes his head like he expected this from me.

Then, suddenly, he does take the edge of my skirt in his hand.

"*Lie down*," he says, tapping the floor. At least, I think that's what he's telling me.

Every part of me grows searing hot. It's instantaneous. Is he going to take me right now?

He looks a little more stern. "*No*," he says as if he can read what I'm thinking right off my face. "*Lie down*."

For some reason, I do it without thinking twice. Once I'm on the floor on his good side, he rolls over to face me. Suddenly our noses are so close together that I could simply lean forward and kiss him. He shifts a little bit so he can reach out with his good arm, and then his fingers go up my skirt.

I don't object. In fact, I lift it up for him, and as his hand ducks underneath, he gets a wry smile that pulls up his tusk on one side. He's surprised when he meets more articles of clothing around my waist. I scoot those off, too, because all I want to know is what he's going to do. He's wearing the same look as he does in the token game when he already has his next devastating move planned. I want to know what he has in mind for me.

And then I'm bare underneath. He can't see what I look like down there, thanks to the skirt, but that doesn't matter when he won't take his eyes off of me. His fingers find their way into the patch of hair between my legs, and then slowly downward, until they're just resting on top of my outer lips.

Can he feel how hot it is down there, how wet I've already gotten for him?

He leans his head even closer, and then, he kisses me.

Blizzek

I don't know why, but I feel like I have to kiss her before I touch her. It's just something I understand, and she eagerly returns the gesture. Her hands find their way into my hair, and her full lips open for me.

But I don't dive in right away, no. I was a favorite with the orcesses and trollesses because I know how to take my time. Maybe I usually get in and get out when I have places to be, but I was a younger orc once who needed to try a little harder to get laid. Instead, I nibble her lower lip and make sure I've explored every corner of it before moving in.

And then, with my tongue in her mouth, I bring my hand into the warm folds between her legs. She lets out a little gasp into me. There I simply run the tip of my finger up and down, lightly nudging her small clit. I can't believe how tiny she is down there. When I gently circle her entrance, wicking away the liquid that's gathered there and then moving up to run it across her clit again, she kisses me harder.

Ah, so that's her turn-on. I had a feeling. Nera is the type who wants it like this—slow and easy.

I couldn't let her leave without returning the favor, especially not after the way she licked me up and down like that. It's clear she's pleased others before me, and for a moment, I think of the man in the painting, covered up by her hand.

I'm even more determined now. There's no reason that a woman like her should have lost someone she loved. I take her mouth harder while I move between her nub and her tiny opening. At first she's merely gasping, but when I put a finger inside of her, she starts to moan. I don't let her have it for long, though, as I start over at the beginning again.

"Blizzek," she groans and releases my mouth. Her eyes are closed and she's holding onto the side of my face like she might disappear if she doesn't. I move faster, harder, and my stitches are straining but I couldn't care less. Her little mewls of pleasure grow higher and higher in pitch, and I want nothing more than to feel her gush on my hand.

And then, she's there, and she has her face pressed to my neck while her little channel seizes around my finger. I can't believe how tight she is. If I ever get to fuck her, I'll never survive.

Nera lies there panting for a time, and I pull my hand out from under her skirt. I lift it to my mouth and take a taste of her, and her eyes go wide.

"*Delicious*," I say. Her smile fills up her whole face.

"*Thank you.*" Her accent is terrible, but I love that she tries.

I get my good arm underneath her head and then pull her closer. Maybe my injuries have worsened a little thanks to this escapade, but it was absolutely worth it. I bury my face in her hair, and suddenly I feel immense relief.

Finally, she's right in the place she's supposed to be.

NERA

Holding me like this, Blizzek says so many things that he wouldn't—and couldn't—say. The way he touches me, slowly and gently at first and then roughly by the end, is like a painting. I can see exactly the kind of lover that he is, this so-called monster in front of me, and it only thrills me for what could come next.

I don't realize that I've fallen asleep like that, wedged up against Blizzek's naked shoulder until it's morning and the sound of his pained groan startles me awake. I blink away the cobwebs in my head and jump right into healer mode.

"*Why?*" I ask.

Blizzek's lying on his back, his brows twisted up in discomfort. I immediately switch to his injured side and look at his wounds. One of them has popped its stitches, and it looks a fierce red.

"Shit," I say to myself. "Got infected."

Last night was not a good plan. I should have known better.

"*I'm sorry,*" I say to him in Trollkin. "*Ouch. Big ouch.*"

He raises his eyebrows, then seems to understand that I've found what's causing his pain—and it will require even more pain to get through it.

I clean the wound again, then Blizzek is covering his side and grunting.

"*It's all right,*" I say, and quickly make up my ingredients. Then I apply it to his wound, and he howls with agony. "*I'm sorry.*"

He shakes his head, then points to himself. He thinks this was his fault, but I enjoyed it just as much.

Once I've taken care of this first step, I have to figure out how to fight his infection. The treatment I need to make doesn't last once it's made so I don't have any stored. I'll have to go get a fresh batch of moss from the riverside, which is a good five miles away. Who knows how close it'll take me toward the battlefield?

I get up to my feet. "*I'm sorry,*" I say in Trollkin. Then, "*Go. Must go.*" I point out the window, and gesture with my hand the sun crossing the sky to the mountains. That's when I should be back.

Blizzek frowns and shakes his head. While I don't understand the words he says, we both know what's out there—a war.

But I have to do it. *"I'm sorry,"* I say again. He calls something else out as I head out the door and close it behind me.

CHAPTER 7

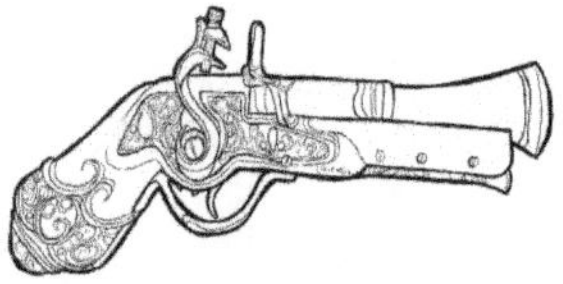

BLIZZEK

Damn it. Now she's going to go out there and risk her life for mine.

I should have probably turned her away when she offered to please me. I should have firmly said *no* because it was bound to get difficult later. I just didn't expect it would happen so soon.

As the hours go by, I watch the sun cross the sky outside like she said, just waiting and waiting. The cat meows at me, then eventually decides to lie down under my good armpit. I really don't mind him, but my thoughts are out there in the woods with Nera.

By the time it's dark, she still hasn't returned. I want nothing more than to get up and go looking for her, but I know if I try it'll only make things worse.

I'm about ready to burst out of my skin when the door finally opens again. It's Nera, and she's panting with effort. Her hair has fallen out of its usual braid and flies wild around her face. She looks like a warrior princess.

"I'm sorry. I have it." She kneels down next to me and starts making up her potion. It's made from some kind of green moss. She adds something else, then continues mixing. Finally, it's a fine paste.

"Ouch," she says again to warn me. I nod and grit my teeth as she starts to rub the mixture all over my blazing-hot wound. I don't let out a cry, but I grunt and strain. Then, she's done.

When I've gotten my breath back, Nera leans over me. "Are you all right?"

"Yes." She looks relieved.

I reach up and touch the side of her face. She went out there in the middle of a war to help *me*. Of everyone in the world, she put herself on the line for my big orc mug. "Thank you."

She reddens a little. "You're welcome."

And it does work. The next morning I feel infinitely better, and my wound is already starting to look like the infection never happened at all. She breathes a deep sigh and wipes her forehead.

"Good." Unfortunately, since she cut my pants off the other night, I'm now buck naked in her house under the blanket. I can see her eyes dart down and then up again, and it gets me thick and eager for her. I vividly remember the feeling of her warm cunt around my fingers, the taste of it on my lips, and I want more than anything to have it again. If I wouldn't be risking my stitches popping open, I would get between her legs and taste the source.

Instead of trying to put clothes on me, Nera decides to sew them together once they're already on my body. I can't imagine how ridiculous I look, but she seems proud of her work, so I say nothing about it.

After that one night, though, we act as if nothing happened. She brings me all of my meals, and I worry that I'm soon going to eat her out of house and home without supplies coming in from outside. She's taken far too good care of me already, much more than I deserve. I don't think I could ever pay her back.

Finally, after what feels like an eternity, I can sit all the way up without stabbing pain. My wounds are now mostly closed, and Nera's taken out my remaining stitches. I know I'll never be quite the same again—there are scars up and down my entire side, for starters—but now I have hope of being able to walk.

Nera comes in from caring for her animals, and her face lights up when she sees me sitting. I pat the seat next to me. She obeys, and instantly I'm kissing her. I simply can't help myself. I need to know what she feels like again under my mouth. All the things I want to do to her—to cradle her naked body, to invade that small cunt of hers, to feel her burst around my cock the way she did around my hand—will have to wait just a bit longer until I'm fully healed.

When I'm fully healed. This thought makes its way into my head, and I pause. Nera pulls away, a perplexed look on her face.

Whenever I'm well enough to fuck, it will be more than time for me to go.

"Blizzek?" she asks. Instead of answering, I kiss her again and revel in the taste of her as much as I can. Some deep part of me is aching, but I crush it under my foot.

NERA

Blizzek doesn't try to get under my skirt as he kisses me thoroughly. No, he simply sighs and brings me close against his chest, and I bury my face in the curve of his neck. He holds me like that for a long time, and I can tell that something isn't right.

But I don't pry. Even though we can communicate a little here and there, I can tell that he's the private sort who keeps all of his cards close in. He cares about me some amount—I knew it the moment I returned home with his medicine and saw the relief on his face. Everything else is a mystery.

After that, Blizzek only gets stronger and stronger, and it feels like a ticking clock. I know that as soon as he's well, that's the end of this, whatever it is; and still, the idea of seeing his back fills me with a heaviness. I try to brush it off—I always knew this was temporary—but for a wistful moment, I want him to turn around and decide to stay, to keep playing the token game with me and kissing me and perhaps doing other things to me.

One day, I'm outside in the garden when I hear the back door open, and I jog around the house to find Blizzek standing there. He squints at the sun and covers his eyes with one hand like a shade.

He's up. A wave of relief washes over me. He survived. I did my job well.

"*Good,*" I say, offering a smile as I walk over, cleaning my hands off on my skirt. "*Very good.*"

When I come to a stop in front of him, he tilts his head down to look into my eyes. There's something soft and velvety in them, and they say more than his mouth ever could.

Though he's still limping a little, it's good for Blizzek to have fresh air again after all that time inside. I show him around the farm, from the sheep pasture to Potato's little stable, and then the sprawling garden where I grow most of the food we eat. He's quiet, taking everything in, his hand occasionally drifting to my back and running down my spine. It seems like an absent, instinctive gesture, and I wonder if he even realizes he's doing it.

When we return to the house, suddenly his arms reach out and grab me around the middle, almost roughly. I gasp as he pulls me in, and then crushes his mouth against mine.

Oh. So this is what it feels like. He's tall, incredibly tall, and I just didn't notice during all that time he spent lying on my floor. I have to stand on my tiptoes just to reach his mouth, but he makes sure to help me. My arms wind around his thick body, his heavy-set chest with the carved muscles, and I fall into him.

And then, suddenly, I'm moving. Blizzek has lifted me off the ground by my rear and is already heading inside with me held tightly in his arms. My breath quickens as I wrap my legs around him. He has some sort of plan. What is he going to do with me?

My question is answered almost immediately as he carries me into my bedroom and sits me down on the bed. He doesn't wait even a second before he starts taking off my shirt, and I'm more than willing to help.

He's going to do it. I didn't think this day would come, and now that it's here, I find myself straddling thrilled and afraid. But I've thought about what he would feel like inside me too many times to refuse him. I want it more than anything.

The moment my shirt is free, his mouth is on my breasts. His tongue is frantic, and I gasp as he sucks my nipple. It's so gentle and yet eager that I melt into Blizzek's huge arms. His hand slips under the band of my skirt, and his finger is hot as it first finds my soft lower lips, then slides inside. He's not wasting any time, not now.

Working one of his four-fingered hands around my breasts, he presses me back against the bed, pumping his hand in and out as I moan and gasp underneath him. Then it's joined by another large finger, and together they're almost too much. It's been a long time since anything of significant size tried to fit inside me, and it takes a few moments for my body to adjust to him.

"Blizzek," I whimper. He tilts my chin up so I'm looking right into his eyes as he prepares me for him, his fingers slicking in and out of my tight channel. When I'm wet and moaning, he peels down my skirt, leaving me naked on the bed in front of him.

"Ah," he says, letting out a puff of air. For just a moment, the look on his face softens as he takes me in, all of me. "*Beautiful.*" I hadn't learned this word before, but his eyes say it all.

He pulls off his shirt, the one I'd sewn in place on him, and then hooks a thumb into his pants and drags them down to his feet. I soak him in as he stands in front of me, huge and rippling with taut muscle, wider than any human man I've ever seen. I hadn't fully realized how thick and heavy and sure he was, lying on the floor for all that time.

And now, his big, deep olive cock is pointed straight at me. I want it more than I've ever wanted anything. Engorged veins run all along it as his body pumps it full of blood, and I wonder what it'll feel like inside me. I'm breathing hard, and before I know it, Blizzek is shoving me down against the bed. When he pulls my knees apart, I know he's exactly what I want.

My breath comes hard and fast as he navigates his huge tip toward the warm, dripping place between my legs. I'm hungering for him. But he doesn't dive in right away, no—he runs just his cockhead around my entrance, collecting all the fluids I've made for him and spreading them around. The crown drags against my clit and I groan, falling back on the bed.

"*Please*," I say in Trollkin. I just want to know what he feels like. "*Please*."

A smile tugs at the edge of his lips, and he leans down to kiss me just as he starts to press inside. I reach out to grab onto his shoulders because I need something to hold onto. I'm stretching for him, desperately trying to accommodate his size, and I let out a moan as my body starts to slowly give.

I want nothing more than for him to sink into me, to finally fill me, but he's going to take his sweet time. Just like I knew he would.

CHAPTER 8

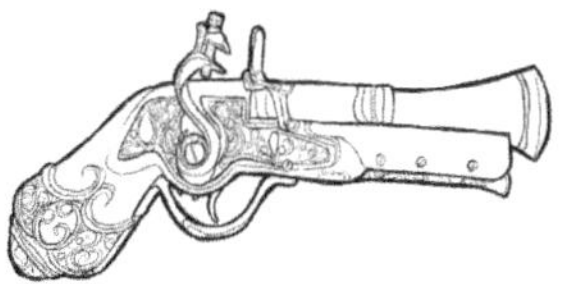

BLIZZEK

She's so unbelievably tight that I have to stop and breathe for a few moments, so I don't come right away.

How long have I been dreaming about this, fantasizing about this, and it's finally here? Nera is so pliable under my hands. Her dark hair lies in a great halo around her head, and her brown eyes are welcoming me inside. Those soft, gentle, kind eyes—they make my heart twist like a rag being wrung out. I want to bring her every kind of pleasure possible. That's my only mission now, before I have to leave her.

I can't let this go any deeper, any longer than necessary, or else I might become bound to her. But I had to do this first.

When I feel Nera start to loosen and widen around my cock, I know it's time. I bury my face in her hair as I start to slide inside. Her entire body tightens up under me as I ease through her tight channel, and the mewl she lets out almost makes me explode on the spot. She's so unbelievably warm, so wet and slippery for me, that I have to bite my lip to hold it all back. No, I'm going to make her scream before I hit my limit.

Letting her tiny sheath accommodate the size of me, I move slowly. I know it's more than she's ever taken, but she only seems to want more and more, wrapping her legs tightly around my waist and pulling me in until I can't resist any longer. I sink my cock as deep in her as it'll go, and she cries out, tangling her hands in my hair. She feels so incredible, so mind-numbingly perfect, that I have to focus hard not to blow my load right away.

Despite how wonderfully she's clenching me, I pull nearly all the way out, and then plunder her again, filling her as full as I possibly can. Though Nera can't take all of me, she feels better than any cunt I've ever been inside. There's a wet, obscene slap as I thrust again, repeating the same complete, slow motion over and over again until she's wound so tight around my cock that I can barely move. She's only making quick, short, high-pitched moans, and her voice is like tinkling bells, growing louder and louder as I keep my slow, steady pace.

I know exactly what she wants, my Nera: A careful, patient, considerate lover, who will draw all that generosity and kindness lying inside her heart up to the surface and hold it tight. Just for now, I will be that lover for her—the kind she deserves. I wrap my arms around her and pull her flush against me as I continue my steady strokes, finding the place deep inside where the curve of me strikes her inner walls. She lets out a cry and buries her face in my collar. Her arms are trembling around me as I find the spot again and again.

"Blizzek," she moans, kissing me ferociously, as if she'll never be able to get enough of me. I try to shove down the massive orgasm building in my hips and kiss her back with the same unspoken truth: This little human woman means the world to me.

Oh, shit. Damn it. It's already happened. The very thing I wanted to avoid has found me.

That's when I feel her sweet, slick cunt start to tighten even more, if that were possible, and she cries out my name. It's the most beautiful music, and I want to hear it forever.

"Are you ready?" I whisper to her, and I don't know if she can understand my meaning, but she nods her head rapidly. Something else is driving me now, this need to bring her as high as I can and claim her as mine. She's clutching me so tight that I know there will be marks on my back. A memento to remember her by.

When I look down into her eyes, she's looking back with an emotion I instantly recognize—she's realized the bond between us now, too. I can feel her soul inside me, wrapping tightly around mine, the two of them melting and merging into one.

No. I didn't want this. I can't even look at her lovely round face. But I've lost control of my body, which is now only driven by my need for sweet Nera. I speed up, shoving through her wet tightness as hard as I can. My small human is screaming now, a full-throated sound that makes my balls tighten knowing that I'm the one doing it to her. I can't control it anymore—I'm swelling up, my cock filling with seed, and her cries grow even more desperate. That's when I feel her channel seize up like a vice around me, and she goes utterly silent. Her eyes roll back, and her fingers clench tighter in my flesh. When I can't move any longer, that's when I know I'm doomed.

I shoot out everything into her. Her entire body is shivering, twitching with pleasure, while I continue gushing. I didn't know I had so much stored up, but it's like my body wants to give her everything it can possibly give. And she takes it, accepting me into her innermost depths and swallowing me.

Fuck. I didn't mean to do that, not inside of her, but it's too late now. I pull out quickly, and she lets out a little surprised—and disappointed—sound. Her tiny slit is covered in my hot seed, as are her smooth, long legs. I'm dripping out of her, and I just shake my head at what I've done.

While Nera lies there panting, her eyes closed in bliss, I get up and start to put my pants back on.

I know that she's expecting me to hold her again, to fall asleep with her head resting against my chest. But if I give that to her, I'll never be able to leave. I will live and die here with her if I don't go *right now*.

"Blizzek…?" she asks, confusion in her voice as she sees me dressing. This is the moment I've been dreading. When I finish putting on my shirt, I look back at Nera, and her eyes are swimming with tears. She knows what I plan to do.

"No." She reaches for me, but I step just out of her grasp. She shakes her head rapidly, and soon the tears are running down her face.

I can't look at her for even a moment longer or I won't have the strength to do what needs to be done. So I turn around and leave.

I hear her sobbing before I'm even out the front door. But I have to keep going. It will hurt now, but she'll thank me later. This had to happen, for both of us.

Nera

Everything about him felt so perfect that I should have known it wouldn't last. I'd predicted from the beginning that this is how it would end, but I didn't think it would be so sudden, so abrupt.

I didn't think it would feel like my heart was being ripped in two.

"Blizzek!" I call his name, but he only stops for a moment in the doorway. His head turns for just a split second as if he might look back at me.

"*Thank you,*" he says quietly, and then he's gone.

The sobs wrack my body, each one ripping itself out. The way he had made love to me... That's what it was. He had made love to me like I was the most precious thing in the world. How could he leave me when he feels that way about me?

I don't understand. Nothing about this makes sense. I have to stop and gasp between sobs because it's almost too much for my body to bear.

I had thought he truly cared about me, but now, there's no way he did. No, he only wanted one thing, and that was to fuck me. And once he got it, he didn't need me anymore.

My devastation starts to morph into anger. It's a strange emotion for me, something foreign and ugly and painful, but I can't help it as it slowly leaks into me, filling me with over-whelming, volcanic heat.

I feel used. The way he wouldn't look at me at the end... I was just an object to him, a convenient hole for his cock. And once he got his fill of it, he was done with me.

I run to the door and, unable to hold all of it inside me anymore, I start to scream. "How could you?! I hate you!"

And then I fall down to my knees and cry.

CHAPTER 9

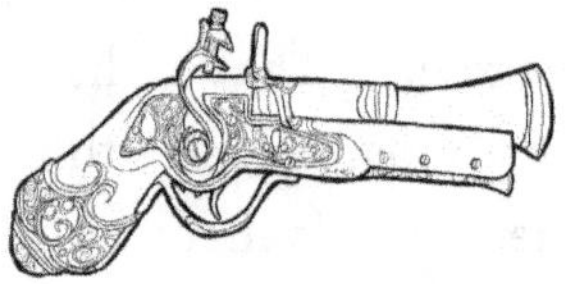

I'm bonded to her—I know it now. I should never have fucked her because all that did was seal the deal.

My mate. I've found her, which means that I absolutely have to go before the bond can get its claws in any deeper.

Behind me, I hear her voice shouting in Freysian. I don't have to understand her language to know she's throwing angry words at my back. I have to steel myself to keep walking. I have to go, find the trollkin camp, and not look over my shoulder at the little house with the garden and the sheep pen. But oh, does it burn, like a fire even greater than when I was pelted with shrapnel.

At least now she hates me. I don't have to leave her with the heartache. Leaving her with rage, with a boiling hatred toward me, is far better. Then she never has to want me, wishing I'll return to her.

Each step is the heaviest step of my entire life, but I take one more, and then one more, and before long Nera's house has disappeared in the trees, and her crying has faded into the distance. I'm not sure which way to go but I keep walking straight, searching for anything I can use to orient myself.

I must have dragged myself quite a long way, riddled with bits of sharpened steel, and then Nera took me another long way more. But after a few miles of trekking, I reach the edge of the trees and gaze upon the burned remains of the town that used to be here. This was where it all happened. Looking at it, I'm not sure who won. The humans may have lost the town, but we lost, too. Our entire front line was obliterated.

I continue walking past decomposing bodies, mostly trollkin but some human, too. At least we took a few of them out with us. But thinking this, seeing their faces, doesn't make me feel good. I imagine the man in the painting as each of them.

I realize that I've gone and broken her heart a second time. I am truly scum.

But I always knew that. She should have known it, too, when she took in an orc she found half-dead in the woods.

When I arrive back at camp, there are only a handful of soldiers around—guards sent to hold down the land we've taken so far. That means the main force has moved on, likely advancing closer and closer toward the humans' capital city. Nera's home is now square in the center of trollkin territory.

But she's managed to survive this long without being detected, far out there in the woods. As long as she stays there, perhaps she'll survive.

I wonder if I've made a terrible mistake by leaving her there. But what else can I do? She's chosen to stay, rather than run. I didn't make that decision for her.

"Who're you?" one of the soldiers asks, getting up off the ground. The troll swaggers over to me. "You look ridiculous."

I sigh. This is going to be difficult. "I got separated from my unit."

The other trollkin exchange looks, and then an orc grunts. "Fancy words for 'deserter'."

The troll laughs, and it's an ugly laugh. "What should we do with him?" The rest of the troupe jeers at me, shouting different ways of stringing me up.

But they're young, weak, and foolish. They were brought in by the conscription, and they have none of the life experience that I do. Before the troll can make his decision over whether or not to attack me, I club him over the head with my fist, then bring up my knee to his abdomen. The orc is next, lunging at me headfirst. I step out of the way, then bring my elbow down into his back. Once the two of them are on the ground, the other three look a little less interested in joining the fray.

"I'll say it again," I grit out. "I got separated from my unit, and I'm trying to find them again."

One of the orcs points off into the distance. "There. Outside the next town. Trying to starve the humans out."

Just great.

After digging out some ragged armor left behind by the former camp occupants, I give the troll one last kick to the side, and he groans. Then I walk away into the woods.

NERA

Once Blizzek has gone, I don't know what to do with myself. I had spent so much time caring for him and keeping him company that now it feels like all I have left is time. I clean until the house is gleaming, then wash all of my clothes. I take care of the sheep and focus on my garden, yanking out the mess of weeds I'd let grow while I was absorbed with my orc.

No. That's not who he is. He was a passerby—just a shadow moving in and out of my life.

At night, though, I can't pretend that it's true. I remember so vividly how he felt, the way he held me close to his chest while he made love to me, right before he left. Now I have an infinite number of hours with which to stew over it, to wallow in my misery and replay every single moment of our time together.

How had he known everything I wanted, down to each stroke? It was like he was inside my mind, pulling up to the surface every carnal desire I'd ever had. I'd felt a pinching deep down in my gut when I started to climax like some unnamed thing inside me had found its home.

And now that thing was torn in half and left on the ground to rot.

Most of all, I can't believe I let it take me by surprise. What did I really think was going to happen between him and me—a human and an orc? I'd been delusional if I thought it would become anything else. He was never going to stay, not once he was better. I knew that all along.

So why had I secretly hoped that he would? I should have known that train would only carry me to heartbreak.

I can't even look at the picture of Refiel anymore. I'm too full of guilt. I fucked this creature in our home because what, he was good to look at? Because I was lonely? Or all of the above?

I got what was coming to me. I can't pretend like getting my heart broken is anyone's fault but mine. Somehow, I just have to forget this ever happened.

But even as I think this, I know there's no way I'll ever forget Blizzek or his short time here, and what he meant to me.

BLIZZEK

Nobody questions it when I rejoin the front line. One member of my unit is still alive, a big orcess with a nasty scar across her face. She doesn't even ask where I've been. Now we're here again all the same.

The trollkin forces have been in the middle of a siege since I left. This fortress is not so easily toppled as the last one—it's built with stone and high walls. Our supplies are running thin. After leaving the little house with the sheepskin rug and the fireplace and the wood beams overhead, sleeping in a damp tent with half the amount of food as typical rations makes me feel like an idiot.

But I had to come back here. This was my only option. I couldn't possibly have stayed with her out in the woods, at the little farm she'd started building with the dead man in the painting. That was a different world, one that I certainly don't belong to. I was an imposter there.

No, sitting out here with the other muddy, shivering trollkin is my fate. I will die along with the others. This is where I was supposed to be at the start.

Suddenly, I think of Raz'jin. Is this the same dizzying misery that he felt when he was separated from his little human mate? It's an ache that claws at me, one that I could never drink away. Not that we have a chance now, starving outside the stone walls of the human city.

Word comes that elsewhere, the trollkin have been pushed back. Our leaders finally withdraw from the siege that we're bound to lose. Instead of pushing ahead, we start staking down our claim in all the neighboring towns that we've burned to the ground. We will defend our stolen holdings and rebuild on top of them.

New battle lines are drawn, and for now, the Great Chieftain's slow progression toward the human capital will halt.

After the ceasefire is called, my unit and I are bustled from one camp to the next, building new guard towers and erecting stone walls to protect our new land. It's worse than a day laborer job—I'm not even getting paid overtime. We work from sunup to sundown. So much for dying on a battlefield. No, I'm going to die in a construction ditch.

Months pass as I work myself nearly raw. But the time is coming that we'll be released, and the conscripted can finally leave and return home if they choose. Part of me considers staying. I deserve the punishment of working my hands to the bone, of spending my life sweating and sore and hungry.

Every day I remember her soft skin under my hands, the taste of her lips underneath mine, and the feeling of her soft, sweet wetness all around me. Whenever I'm deep in this memory-fantasy, I look up and find her big, brown eyes staring deeply into mine, calling me back home.

Suddenly, the decree comes down: Conscription has ended, and we're free to go.

My first instinct is to go back to find Nera, to warn her that she's now firmly in the middle of enemy territory. But it would only harm her to enter her life again—it might even lead them to her. No, that would be self-serving. The right thing to do is to go back to Kalishagg. It's my home, or has been since I set out on my own as a young, dumb orc whelp. I know the bartenders, the women, the shop keeps, and the other regulars.

I'm paid meager wages for my conscription time. Without thinking twice about it, I take the money and buy my ticket back home.

But when I get to the city of Kalishagg, everything looks different. It's all uglier, and the smell has changed to something foul. Suddenly I can't stand it. The hustle and bustle fills me with a new, fresh kind of anxiety, and all I can think about are shrapnel bombs going off, everyone around me falling down dead, and the dismembered tip of a sword lodged in each of their throats. Every loud sound—a horse's hoof on stone streets, a hammer banging into an anvil—makes me jump.

I can't stay here. Without Raz'jin alongside me while I drink away my misery, remaining in the hot stink of Kalishagg just doesn't feel right. So I decide to board a boat, any boat, and see where it might take me that's far away from here.

I go from place to place for months, searching for veins of gold and silver to sell. I'm reminded again of Raz'jin, of the pair we used to be before the war took our souls. Soon, I'm heading out to the Frattern Islands on a boat I'd chosen at random. As a neutral territory, it's thriving in this post-war state. More people than ever are flocking there to trade and travel. Once upon a time, Raz'jin had spoken of emeralds hiding in the sand on the islands. Perhaps I could brave the coastal rain and go searching for my fortune, too.

But it's not the emeralds that pull me there. I need to lose myself in something. I need to understand what he found, what he saw out here, that changed him so fundamentally— that made him into the troll I didn't recognize afterward.

Besides, I can't possibly sink further down from here. There's nowhere left to go.

CHAPTER 10

Things have changed. I can sense that much just from standing at my front door. The very air vibrates with it.

I simply can't survive on sheep's cheese and greens any longer, and it's long past time to get supplies. As the months go by, the sense of encroaching danger is slowly penning me in from all sides. I know in my gut that going out now is risking discovery and death.

And so when they do find me, I'm not surprised. It was only a matter of time.

While I'm out working, I hear a deep, gruff voice calling out in Trollkin. They've spotted my sheep, probably figuring they'd secured their next meal. Before they can catch sight of me in the garden, I sprint inside the house. I try to keep my thoughts straight even though the panic is worming its way into me. Maybe I can lead them to believe the house is abandoned. I grab my hand axe before heading out the front door, where I immediately start to run.

"*Human!*" a voice calls out. I know that word.

Shit. I pick up my pace and dart around trees, but I can hear footsteps crunching leaves and twigs not far behind me. If they're anything like Blizzek, these trollkin are bigger and faster and much stronger than I am. Unless I can get clever and lose them, I don't stand a chance.

I run past a deep thicket where I come foraging for blackberries, and rather than continuing on, I loop back around it. I dive into the bush, and nearby, I hear footsteps thundering past. The trollkin are yelling at each other, "*Human! Over there!*"

I remain completely silent, trying to still my trembling. And then, the footsteps recede. They assume I ran off into the woods and will pursue me in that direction for some time. The powerful pulsing of my blood starts to slow down, and I take deep breaths to help me focus on what comes next.

I can't go back to the house now. The others are probably pillaging my cellar as we speak and cutting down my sheep for mutton. I hope Arri hears the commotion and gets out safely.

Everything I built with Refiel will be pillaged, ruined, and stripped bare.

Maybe I have a chance of getting out of trollkin-controlled territory alive if I can stay quiet, move slowly, and keep my eyes peeled. Perhaps I can make my way to the capital city, about sixty miles from here. It's risky, but I have no choice now.

After a few minutes hearing no noise outside my little hiding place, I step out of the bushes and look around. That was a close call. Who knows what the trollkin would have done to me when they captured me? I wonder if I'd have become a thrill kill, a slave, or worse—a concubine. I feel cold at the thought.

Then, a hand lands on my shoulder. It's heavy and strong, with only four fingers. It closes around me, and I can't help the shriek I let out.

The massive, unfamiliar orc smiles down at me, but it's not a friendly smile. "*Found you.*"

I don't try to fight him as he ties my hands around my back and tosses me over his shoulder, pain shooting through my diaphragm. Struggling will only get me killed faster. As painful as life has been since Blizzek left, I still want to live. Maybe if I do, I'll have the chance to see him again.

Where will this monster take me? What horrors will I face now? I can't help the tears that start to stream down my face.

Carrying me under one arm like a sack of flour, my captor reunites with the others. I can only make out a few of the words, but I get the gist. There's a camp nearby and they're taking me with them. I was foolish—so foolish—to stay here for so long. Now I will suffer for it.

A huge troll takes possession of me and carries me a few miles to a muddy camp, where dirty orcs and trolls and even one big ogre are assembled, all of them covered in mud and obviously miserable. It's like I thought: They don't want to be here as much as we don't. But creatures that have sunk this low will seek to push others even lower. They will be cruel and harsh masters. I'm shivering by the time we reach the cages on the far end of camp. I know as soon as I see them that I'm destined for one. I don't even struggle as the troll puts me down, opens one of the doors, and shoves me inside.

"*Good,*" he says. "*Don't fight, and this will go better for you.*"

I nod. "*I understand,*" I respond in Trollkin. The troll looks at me, aghast. Then he shakes his head, and he's gone.

I move away from the door, keeping my knees bent because

of the low ceiling of the cage, and look around at my new surroundings. There are two other humans here with me, each crammed into a separate corner. They look up at me as I join them but don't speak. They're just as filthy as the soldiers, and they are painfully scrawny. Surely prisoners are the last on the list when it comes to distributing rations. I'd better prepare myself for going hungry a lot.

As I find my place in one of the corners of the cage, I try not to let the fear and misery inside me. It won't help to go down the path of self-pity, because that will only make this all worse. No, I need to believe that somehow, this is how things are supposed to be and I will make it out alive.

I have to. There's simply no other option.

BLIZZEK

Eyra Cove is a living, breathing organism. When my ship docks and the ramp drops down, I'm overwhelmed by the color and sound of it. Creatures of all kinds have converged on this one place. Ships wait at almost every pier, while passengers come and go from the wood walkways connecting the city's shops, taverns, and even brothels together.

It's summer in the Frattern Islands, and the blue-green water is quiet and warm. Perhaps I made the right decision to come here after all. I have money to spend before I have to find more work, and this is a far better place to waste away in a bar, drinking myself under the table, than Kalishagg. Maybe I could even get lucky and find another human woman to fuck and try to pretend she's my Nera instead.

While that likelihood is incredibly low, there's no harm in hoping, is there?

The first thing I need to do is buy some new clothes. I'm still wearing my ragged, beaten uniform, which isn't a great look in a neutral city like Eyra Cove. It makes me appear like I'm out for blood, and the guards are already keeping a steady eye on me as I make my way to the row of shops up on the second level.

Everything you could possibly want is here, just waiting to be purchased at a fair price: Weapons, armor, exotic food, trinkets, and toys—a perfect one-stop shop. I desperately want a new gun to replace my old blunderbuss, which I lost early in the war, but that would eat up most of my funds. Tech isn't cheap. Instead, I buy a rough sword and some new chain armor. I'm not going to leave myself exposed again.

When I reach the leather shop, I pause to examine a pair of boots. They're solid and heavy, and they would last me for years.

"You can try them on," says a human woman behind the counter. She's speaking fluent Trollkin. "Make sure they fit. If they don't, I'm happy to alter them, or custom make you a pair."

When I look up at the shop keep, I could swear that I've seen her before. She has bright orange-red hair, sharp green eyes, and skin smattered with freckles. When I've been staring at her for an awkwardly long time, not speaking, she squints.

"Wait. I think I—" Before she can finish, a little squawk coming from somewhere in the back interrupts her. She sighs. "One second." The woman gets up and walks into an adjoining room. "You want to sit with Mom for a while?" she asks someone and then returns with...

A troll whelp? It has blue skin, four fingers, and just a faint hint of tusks beginning to grow from its little mouth. She cradles it in her lap. "Sorry about that," she says as the little whelp snuggles into her chest. "Anyway. I was just thinking that you look familiar."

Everything clicks into place at once. It's her—Raz'jin's human. The sharp green eyes are what finally tip the scales, and the creature in her arms is, most certainly, his whelp.

I lean toward her, and nervously, she leans away. "Raz," I say quietly. "Is he here?"

Perhaps he got her pregnant right before he died. That's all I can think because I can't get my hopes up that he survived.

"I thought that was you." A huge smile takes over her face. "You're his friend, right? I'll go get him." As she stands up, the little whelp starts to cry, and, with another sigh, she holds him close. "Shh, Izzek. It's fine."

My heart comes to a complete stop.

"Oh, right," she says, turning to me. "Raz did name him after you. He thought you were dead, you know." Every single thought has fled my mind as the human woman turns away and heads back into the shop, calling out, "Raz! Someone's here to see you!"

"Huh?"

I would know that voice anywhere. It's him—it's really him. A door closes and like magic, the troll Raz'jin appears, walking with a limp. When he sees me, his mouth falls open. "Blizzek?"

"You're alive." I almost don't know what to do. Trollkin aren't really the hugging type, but I'm so overjoyed at seeing him that I consider it. Instead, he holds out a hand and I shake it with ferocious enthusiasm.

"So are you," Raz says. He grins mischievously at me. "But you always were a slippery bastard, weren't you? I shouldn't be surprised you got out without even a scratch."

I shake my head and lean to one side, pulling up my shirt to show off my maze of scars. Raz's eyes widen. "Damn," he says. "You got lucky."

He has no idea how lucky.

"Wait," I begin, "you have a—"

Raz'jin quickly interrupts me. "We have a lot to talk about. Let's get out of the way so Telise can work." The human woman reappears, the little whelp eagerly sucking her breast.

There's just no fucking way.

"Go," she says, gesturing at us to leave. "Catch up. I'll watch him."

I have no words, really, as Raz'jin leads us away up a flight of stairs.

He's really alive—and there's clearly a lot more to it than that.

Chapter 11

Nera

I'm not sure how much time passes in that cage. Each day is longer than the one before it, until it feels like the sun rising, crossing the sky, and setting again takes a whole year. The other humans talk occasionally, but the trollkin feed us so little (and what they do feed us is filthy and nearly inedible) that we don't have much energy for it. My stomach has stopped rumbling with hunger, and now it aches almost all day and night.

Most of the humans were captured in the fighting and have been rotting away here for months. I feel guilty that I wasn't there with them on the front lines. I've just been hiding out in the woods for who knows how long, hoping none of this would find me. That was delusional, I realize now. I should have left when Blizzek did and joined the war effort. I'm no fighter, certainly, but it was my responsibility, and I shirked it.

Now I'm here, reaping the rewards.

We aren't left in the cages forever. I'm actually thankful

when they take us out and chain us together, then put us to work—for a few hours, at least. I'm weak, so the first couple of days working out in the hot sun, under constant pressure from the taskmaster, render my muscles nearly unusable. I'm sore in places I've never been sore before, but there's no time to rest, as each day they put us back on the line. It seems like we're building a new town right where the human one lay in ashes.

Soon one of the other prisoners develops a bad rash from the chains around our ankles. If left untreated, it could spread up her leg and eventually take her foot completely. I do what I can to help, but I have no supplies.

"*Please*," I ask one of the guards who keeps an eye on us. I gesture at my neighbor. "*Help her.*" The troll is so surprised to hear me using Trollkin that he doesn't respond at first.

"*Just a prisoner*," he says, and waves me off.

But I'm not so easily dissuaded. "*She will die*," I tell him. Then what use would she be to them? He eyes me, clearly suspicious of my motives. I gesture at the forest. "*I can fix*," I say. I've been steadily picking up more Trollkin as time goes on, listening in on as many of their conversations as possible. "*I find, yes?*"

He shakes his head. "*No way.*" They're not going to let me out of their sight, of course.

"*Please*," I ask again. "*Go with me.*" Maybe if they know I'm not trying to take off on my own, they'll let me forage for the plant I need.

With a look of extreme annoyance on his face, the troll sighs and walks away. I assume that's the end of it. I turn to the woman with the bad foot.

"Sorry," I say. "I tried."

"You speak Trollkin?" She seems more suspicious of me now than anything.

I shrug, and the work continues on. Prisoners aren't the

only ones laboring—the trollkin have enlisted their own conscripts to help build, too. They just aren't chained together.

The sun is high in the sky and I'm sweating bullets when the troll from earlier returns. He grabs me by the wrists and unchains me from the group. A few of the other prisoners shoot me deadly looks—as if I'm getting some kind of special treatment.

"I'll go with you," the troll says. He ties my wrists together with a rope and takes the long end in his hand. *"Now get to it. And don't think of running off."*

I nod eagerly and lead him away into the woods.

Neither of us says anything as I search for the plant I need. It has a bright orange flower that should be easy to spot from a distance. Soon I catch sight of a bit of swamp up ahead, and the plant I'm after likes to grow where there's lots of water. Pulling on the rope, I gesture to the reeds scattered all around the edges. *"There,"* I say. *"Go there."*

And thankfully, I'm right. As we wade into the swamp, I spot the orange flower I'm looking for and excitedly say, *"That. That."*

Curious, the troll leans down and picks the plant. I hold out my hands for it, and then we're walking back the way we came at a quick clip.

When we get back to camp, the troll lets me lead the way to the objects I need: A bowl, a rock, and some water. Quickly I take the plant apart and drop what I need into the bowl, then mix it up into a paste.

"Here," I tell the woman, indicating to her leg. "This will help."

I rub the rash down and she hisses in pain, but I promise her that it will be worth it. Once I'm finished, the troll puts me back on the line with the other prisoners, and we continue our work. But I can tell that afterward, the trollkin are watching me more carefully, as if afraid I'll try to run off if given the chance.

The next morning, the woman's rash is already beginning to recede. She flexes her ankle.

"Not bad," she says. "How did you know to do that?"

"My father was a healer. He taught me everything he knew."

She smiles with appreciation, but none of us have the energy for words of gratitude.

Later that day, the troll from before returns to examine the foot. He notes that the remedy has worked, and leaves without a word. I believe that's the end of it.

A few days later, an orc that I don't recognize approaches me. He's wearing an insignia—he must be of a higher rank than a mere grunt. He grabs my arm and pulls me away from the line, disturbing the prisoners to either side. They glare at me.

"*You.*" The orc narrows his eyes. "*You're the healer?*"

I nod. Without any more questions, he removes my chains, tying me up with a rope the same way as before. He drags me along behind him through the muddy camp—where he's taking me, I have no idea.

We come to a sudden stop in front of a small fire, where another orc lies prone on a bed of dirty furs. He has dark spots all over his skin and his breathing is labored.

"*Healer,*" my escort says, pointing at me. "*She can help.*"

Can I? He has a disease I've only seen once before, and I'm fairly certain it comes from living in filthy conditions, just like those all around us. The best I can do would be to treat his symptoms and hope that he can go home soon.

"*He's sick,*" I say. I gesture around at the mud. "*I can't fix.*"

The orc holding my rope snarls at me. "*Aren't you a healer?*"

I nod and try to explain as best I can with the limited

amount of Trollkin available to me that he won't get better unless he leaves—but I can help in the meantime.

"*Fine,*" the orc says irritably. But his green-gold eyes are fastened on me, intent on me. "*Then help.*"

We repeat the same process as before: I'm handed off to the same troll grunt, then we go out into the woods and wander around until I find what I need. I'm missing some important components, though, and it won't work without them.

"*My house,*" I say. "*I need my house.*"

"*House?*" The troll does not look pleased with this.

"*It's not far.*"

Luckily, I've earned a little goodwill with this guy, so he lets me lead the way the few miles through the woods. I know this forest like the back of my hand, so it's not long before I spot the telltale fences where my sheep used to live. They're all gone, of course—butchered for rations long ago.

I lead him inside, and I'm surprised to find my house is still mostly in the state I left it. The larder has been raided, but I expected that. Arri is nowhere to be found.

Good. The last thing I need is this troll deciding my cat would make a good dinner.

I locate my old medicine cabinet and thankfully, it hasn't been touched. A lot of my supplies are expired now, but I have everything that I need to treat the orc back at camp. I remember when Blizzek lay on my floor, and I used every technique in my arsenal to make sure that he would survive.

I pull out everything and gesture to the troll. "*Bring this,*" I say.

He scowls. "*That's too much.*"

"*I need it.*" I don't, of course, but having it means I can treat any other conditions that might come up. It's not like it's going to any use here.

"*Fine.*"

I find a basket I once used for bringing in produce from my garden and fill it up. Then we're headed back the way we came.

Maybe if I prove useful, I can find some way out of here—or stumble across some opportunity to escape. That's the most I can hope for.

BLIZZEK

"How did you make it out alive?" It's the first question I ask because I was sure Raz'jin had died in the assault on the fortress like the rest of our unit.

"Telise found me." He looks far away as he says it. "She was there, too—dragged into that horrible fucking war."

After everything they'd been through, I'm genuinely surprised that he didn't kill the human once he saw her again.

"Oh, I wanted to," Raz says when I ask. "But you'll find that she's very, very persuasive."

He explains to me how this very place—Eyra Cove—was where he realized the little redheaded human was his mate. I figured as much. And now, it's the only place where such an unlikely couple as the two of them feel safe to live.

"I can't believe you had a kid," I say. "That you even *could* have a kid. You, a dad? That's just fucked up." He knows I'm joking, though, and simply smiles. It's a peaceful, truly happy kind of smile, and for some reason, it stabs a dagger right through my heart.

"I had to work pretty hard at it," he says with a booming laugh. "The powers that be don't make it easy to knock up a human, but it is possible."

Instantly I remember fucking Nera and letting every last drop of me shoot inside her. Dread slithers into my stomach, and then my chest. The horror must show on my face because Raz's eyebrows draw together in concern. "Blizz? What is it?"

My mouth opens and closes silently because I have no idea what to tell him.

I might have also knocked up a human, who I'm certain is my mate. Oh, and then I left her behind.

But if there's anyone in this entire stupid world to whom I could tell the truth, it would be Raz, the kinky deviant who's married a human and built a strange little family with her.

"Well," I begin. "You weren't the only one out on that battlefield who barely made it out."

And I explain the entire sordid story. How Nera found me and took me to her home to nurse me back to health. How she fed and clothed me. How I bonded to her—wanted nothing but her—and I was fairly certain I'd imprinted on her. That was how I knew that I had to leave her.

"Wait, what? Why did you have to leave?" Raz looks puzzled.

"She's human! And she lives in the middle of a war zone."

"So... Then you abandoned her in the middle of that war zone alone?"

Each of his questions is making me angrier than the previous one.

"I'd only have put her in danger," I say with a growl. "If anyone found me, I'd have been hanged as a deserter, and then who knows what would have happened to her."

"Or you'd have fought them off. I know you, Blizz. You wouldn't let a few scouts take you down, not without a fight."

"They would have come across us eventually."

"Then why not leave with her?"

He's poking holes in my walls faster than I can put up new ones.

"You don't get it," I snarl. "It would never have worked. The odds against us were too great. She didn't need me coming and ruining her life by taking her as mine."

But Raz just looks sad. He was never this raw with his emotions before—it must be that little human's doing that he seems to suddenly be all feelings.

"What?" I scowl at him. "Are you pitying me?"

"Sure, a little. You missed out on something that could've been really great." He sighs and leans against his elbow. "I get how much it hurts right now, you know. I've been there before."

I want to throw it back in his face and shout that he can't possibly understand what I'm going through. How could he grasp the measure of this exquisite, bone-deep pain? But then I remember that in fact, he has been there. I watched him suffer through it firsthand, and I had no sympathy for him then. I didn't believe that "mates" even existed, especially not with a human.

"I did it to myself," is all I can say.

Raz just nods and finishes throwing back his beer. "Yeah, you did. But that doesn't mean it's too late."

"It is too late," I say with conviction. "Even if I went back, she wouldn't forgive me."

My friend just watches me with an open kind of curiosity. "If she's your true life mate, she would forgive you for anything. Once upon a time, I wanted nothing more than to kill Telise myself. She betrayed me. She hurt me deeper than anyone ever has. But look where I am now."

We get up from the bar and head back to the shop. Raz shows me the little house he's built off the back, and on his way in, he snatches up Izzek and carries him along on the tour.

"He looks like your regular whelp," I say, watching the boy as Raz sits me down at the table.

"Surprising, huh? He's like a copy of me."

"You're sure your tiny human is the mother?" I ask, still disbelieving.

He grins widely at this. "Yep. I watched him come out."

I shudder at the image, shaken right to my core.

"Not sure if that's how it always is," Raz continues, "but I think he's our lone experiment. Can't seem to get her pregnant again."

"You're *trying*?" I barely recognize the guy in front of me.

"Sure—hard as I can. But nothing sticks." He sighs as Izzek starts grabbing things off the table and playing with them. "Once you find your mate, you know, that's all you'll want to do. It's built-in."

I don't even have words for how I feel. Suddenly, I hate myself. I hate who I am so deeply that I wish I could throw myself off a bridge into a pit full of spears. Raz watches me as each of these thoughts runs through my head.

"That way you're feeling right now, Blizz? It doesn't have to be like that." He has to take away a little butter knife that Izzek's gotten his tiny sausage fingers around. "Just go back. Risk everything. It'll be worth it."

I watch as my friend lifts up his child and carries him away from the table. "Can't take you anywhere," Raz mutters as he kneels on the floor and grabs a little wooden train. "What about this one, huh? You like this one." The whelp takes the train and immediately shoves the whole thing in his mouth. Raz just sighs. "Yep. That's a favorite, all right." He leaves the kid on the floor as he comes back to the table.

Seeing him like this... Some part of me that I never knew even existed is aching. It's searing a hole right through me, and I can't fucking stand it.

I have to get back to her.

When I get up from the table abruptly, Raz'jin has an annoying little twinkle in his eye. "Heading out?" he asks.

"I'm done here. Got what I needed." I make my way to the door. "Raz, I'm glad that you lived."

"Same." He gives me a dumb grin. "Now go make sure that you do, too."

He's always been a little smug, but not this smug.

On my way out, his human waves at me. "It was good to actually meet you this time, Blizzek," she says. "Didn't get as good a look at you when you had a gun to my head."

"Take care of him," I say. I noticed my friend's rather significant limp earlier. I suppose surviving the war didn't come without its price.

"Always." She looks back at her customer and I take off, heading down to the pier as fast as I can.

CHAPTER 12

NERA

The orc with the spotted skin does get better, at least enough to be back on his feet. I recommend again that they send him home to properly recover, and after some debate, they agree.

Once more, I return to the other prisoners. They murmur about me cozying up to our captors, but the woman with the rash—who's almost completely healed by now—shuts them up.

More days pass working out in the sun, struggling to lift heavy logs and sweating until I'm certain there's no more water left in my body. Every day my mind drifts back to those days at my house nursing Blizzek back to health. I replay each moment over and over: The way I fell asleep on his shoulder. How he looked the day I took off his clothes and he lay naked on my floor, his cock alert and ready for me. I remember the way he made sure that I was wet for him, how he slid inside me, so perfectly fitted to my body—and worked so hard to please me. I remember when he looked into my eyes, and I saw just how he felt about me.

It wasn't one-sided. It was all there then, and so his leaving still doesn't make sense to me.

I'm not angry anymore. No, I'm glad that I had him as long as I did, so I could know what it's like to feel this way about another creature before I die out here. It seems impossible that I won't see him again. I wish I could tell him what he meant to me for those few weeks we spent together, because it's everything. Every day I try to hold these feelings, these memories, tight against me to keep the helplessness and the desperation at bay.

One night, the orc with the insignia approaches our cage. He has a thick, ornamental fur around his neck, and I think he's probably high up on the ladder here in this sprouting village. He opens the door and points at me. "You. Come now."

I don't argue. This is likely just another job, another sick trollkin to heal. I can manage that. I feel the other prisoners' eyes on me as he grabs me by the arm and drags me out of the cage, then I'm tied up once more and led away, deep into the camp.

The trollkin are rowdy tonight, a bonfire blazing at the center of their raucous gathering. Many leer at me as I pass, and I hope that my captor doesn't decide to hand me over. They shout things I don't understand, things that are clearly obscene, and one of the trolls lobs some spit at me. The orc escorting me stops, turns around, and bashes the troll right in the head. Everyone else around the fire goes deadly silent.

Whoever this orc is, he's certainly the one in charge.

But instead of being taken to an ailing patient, I'm led to a huge tent. A prickle of fear starts at the base of my neck. The orc with the insignia stops at the door and nods to the armed guards.

"Don't interrupt us," he growls and opens the door flaps.

Horror descends on me. Standing out was foolish. Now this orc has taken a shine to me, and being chosen is never a good thing.

My legs don't move when he pulls me through the door. I stumble and fall to my knees. None of my limbs are working as I imagine what comes next, inside this tent alone with him.

"Get up." The orc yanks on the rope again, and I manage to get back to my feet and follow him inside, my blood pumping furiously.

There's a little fire burning in a brazier in the middle of the tent. In the corner is a bed dressed in luxurious-looking furs, and next to it, a desk covered in inks and quills. All of these run-of-the-mill, everyday items are screaming *warning! Warning!*

The orc finally stops and ties me to one of the wood posts holding up the tent, and I wonder if I can convince him not to do this. He walks away, still not speaking, then starts to take off his armor. The movements are mechanical, practiced, as he removes one piece of gear at a time and hangs it off a rack in the corner.

And then his chest is bare, and something about seeing his muscled back stirs a place in me I thought I'd forgotten about. Blizzek. I remember how he looked when I peeled off his shirt. Even sick and stitched up, he was beautiful, and I wanted nothing more than to touch him.

"Do you like what you see?" a deep voice asks.

I realize that I've been staring at this orc who is definitely not Blizzek and envisioning someone else in his place. No, when he turns around, this one has three huge scars across his front like he got into a fight with a lion and barely won. He is not my orc.

"N-no." I turn my head away. "I'm sorry."

He arches an eyebrow and takes a step toward me. "How did you learn to speak our language?"

I don't understand all of what he says, but I get the point. And yet I don't know how to answer his question in a way that won't encourage him even more. This is not the time to admit that you have, in fact, fucked an orc before. But I don't know what lie I would tell, either.

"An orc," I say eventually.

This earns a deeper interest. "One of us taught you?" He narrows his eyes. "Why?"

Why indeed? Because I tried. I wanted to communicate with him, and he accepted my peace offering.

"I healed him," I say.

My captor thinks about this for a long time, his expression giving away nothing. Then he turns back to the racks and resumes taking his clothes off. I turn my head politely as he pulls down his pants. I can't look, not at this. I won't look no matter what.

While I keep my head turned, I expect his hands on me any moment—but after a while, I hear him clear his throat. When I open my eyes, he's changed into a pair of soft sheepskin breeches.

"First you look, and then you look away," he says. "Pick one." He sits down on his huge bed and starts to rub his feet. "You healed him, you were saying?"

How is he so calm about this while my panic is growing? What is he after here?

"Hurt," I say. "He was hurt."

"Hmm." The orc thinks about this. Then, as if he's had a brilliant idea, he walks over and unties me. When he starts to pull me toward the bed, my feet stick to the floor. I won't let him force himself on me, not without a fight. My stomach is rolling. Annoyed, he pulls again, but I resist. I'm not getting anywhere near that bed.

"Don't, please," I whimper. "I'll heal anyone you want if you don't—"

"Quiet." I fall silent and look up. The orc just looks irritated with me. "I'm not going to fuck a disgusting human."

He pulls again and I take a step, then another step, until he's sitting on the bed and I'm right in front of him. Then he leans close and unties the rope.

"Don't run off," he says. "You won't make it."

I swallow and nod. I have no illusions about getting past him or the guards outside.

Then he holds out a foot toward me and gestures to it. When I don't move, he shakes his foot and growls impatiently. "You're a healer, aren't you? Then heal."

Oh. That's all he wants? My relief is immeasurable.

I kneel down and take his foot in my hands, then slowly start to rub it. Maybe if I can do this well and keep him happy, he won't decide to tear off my clothes. So I work each of the muscles, digging gently into the flesh and then smoothing it over. The orc leans back on the bed and lets out a little groan of pleasure.

Once I'm finished with both feet, I pull my hands away. He doesn't move for a long time, but when he does, he's watching me with shadowed eyes.

"Did you do that kind of 'healing' on him, too?" he asks, and I can hear a hint of jealousy in his voice. Maybe I didn't rub Blizzek's feet exactly, but I think of lying side-by-side on the floor and swallow.

The huge blush that rises into my face must give me away immediately because the orc scowls. "I thought so. There would be no reason to teach a human the civilized tongue unless you were bedding her."

I turn away and stare down at the floor. This conversation is not going in a good direction.

"Well, I think that makes you even more perfect for the task I have in mind for you." He flexes his toes and sighs again.

"I won't do it," I say. "I will fight." If anyone but Blizzek comes near me that way—I will kick and scream until I am blue in the face. I will scratch and bite.

He reaches forward and grabs me by the collar of my shirt, and suddenly, his expression has shifted to anger. "Must I repeat myself?" he asks in a low, threatening voice. "I will not soil myself with a human. Whoever this other orc is—he's committed a crime against his people." He tosses me back to the floor, and I catch myself before I skid into a post.

The relief crashes over me like cool water. I don't even mind the rough treatment.

"So what do you want me for?" I ask.

The orc smirks down at me. "Well, little human... You are going to be my personal slave."

BLIZZEK

It takes so long. The time traveling back across the ocean feels like months, even years. And then there's the dreary, uncomfortable trip by wagon toward the edge of what is now orc territory, bumping over rocks and dips in the uneven road.

I have no sane reason to be here, at what used to be the front lines. I was conscripted and released—I shouldn't want to come near this place ever again.

But I have to find her. I need to tell her the truth. I need to have her back again, if she'll even consider it. Nothing makes more sense to me right now. Maybe someday, I could have a life like Raz'jin's.

Before all of this, such an idea would have been utterly ridiculous. Now, the fierce hunger in my heart threatens to choke me. I need her in my arms again. I'm desperate to look into her eyes while I fuck her over and over, making her moan and scream and come around me. Once wasn't enough—no, I need to sink into her, to fill her up with me, for the rest of my life. I want to see her fat with my whelps. Nera would be an incredible mother, I think.

Settlers have already begun traveling out this way, ready to help build the new frontier. They'll take over all the former human homes and farms and put down roots, and it's only a matter of time before they find Nera's homestead out in the woods.

I don't know where we'll go, but she can't stay here any longer. Somehow, I have to convince her to leave—even if it's not with me.

I thought I'd have forgotten how to get to her little home deep in the forest, but my feet lead me right there. I stop and stand outside the human house where Nera brought me, all on her own, and took me in like I was one of her kind.

Swallowing down my nerves, I walk up to the front door and bring up my fist to knock. What will she do when she sees me again? Will she scream obscenities at me? I deserve that, of course. But I will get her away from this place, whether she comes willingly or whether she kicks and shouts. If the other trollkin find her and take her... I don't want to imagine what would happen.

We don't treat the humans we take captive well, at the very least.

Finally, I bring my knuckle down against the door—and it creaks right open, like it wasn't even closed properly. Perhaps

Nera just forgot. She is forgetful from time to time, and sloppy, too. I think of her skirt, covered in stains of every kind, and smile.

The door swings open. When no voice comes from inside, I push it wide and step through.

The house looks almost the same as before—the sheepskin rugs, the little bedroom, the table with the ink and quill on it. But the ink has been knocked over and drips off the side of the table onto the floor.

Nera wouldn't allow that, not on her precious floor. This whole house is her baby.

A little worm of fear starts working its way up from my belly. I walk through the living room where I once lay on the floor, and I stop at the wide-open medicine cabinet. Inside, everything is gone.

Maybe she left of her own volition. That would be good. Perhaps she found out that trollkin had taken over this territory, and it was time to go before they could find her. That would explain why she took all of her supplies.

But something still stinks. I look inside her bedroom, and all of her clothes are right where they used to be inside her drawers. She would've taken those with her, right? None of her blankets have been disturbed. For a woman on the run, these things don't make sense together.

In the kitchen, the larders have been emptied out and the cupboards thrown open.

That's when I hear a little mewl down by my feet. A cat rubs up against my calf and starts to purr.

It's Arri, Nera's beloved companion. I kneel down and he's eager to be petted, as if he hasn't had any attention in weeks.

She wouldn't leave without Arri. The dread is building, swelling, filling up my entire chest. Everything looks wrong.

I step out into the backyard, carrying the cat in one arm,

and survey what's left. The garden is full of produce that has all rotted. She would've taken that with her, too. The barn where she housed her horse is empty, but the wagon is still there.

The pens are littered with the bones of sheep. Every last one of them—butchered.

They found her, and they took her, leaving only the cat behind.

I'm so angry at myself that I'm temporarily blinded. Raz was right. I left her to the wolves. I imagine my Nera, filthy and bruised, tied up to a row of other prisoners. Back when I was conscripted, the human captives were forced to work right alongside us. In my mind's eye, she's one of them.

The roar comes out of me before I can stop it. Arri springs from my arms and hides behind the barn as my fury echoes around the trees.

I have to find her and undo what I've done.

CHAPTER 13

NERA

The guards call him Lieutenant Agkar. There's a pile of furs for me now set up in the opposite corner of his tent, and he demands that I sleep there so I can be at his beck and call.

I don't even try to fight it because there's no reason to. I'm on my own here, and there's no way out. Even if I tried to run, I would never make it past the walls I helped erect all around the outside of the village.

Lieutenant Agkar makes me rub his feet, get his water, and from time to time, I even have to bathe him. He never insists I wash him between the legs, and for that, I'm deeply grateful. No longer do I have to work on the line—now I have clean clothes and a soft, warm place to sleep. But guilt rakes at my heart, to have this luxury while the other humans toil outside. I was given a second chance in Agkar's tent, and in comparison to theirs, my life is like that of royalty.

Sometimes I'm taken away to work my healer's hands on

trollkin who have fallen ill or suffered an injury. Once I prove that I'm not about to run away anytime soon, Agkar doesn't tie me up at night. Eventually, he even lets me move around the camp on my own, getting things I need—ingredients for meals that I make for him, or a needle and thread to fix holes in his clothes. He treats me more or less like a piece of furniture, undressing in front of me, even masturbating in his bed while I'm in the tent with him. A ball of heat settles between my legs, imagining it's Blizzek on that bed instead. I remember every time I gave him a raging erection. I think of how he felt buried up to the hilt inside me.

Blizzek. That feels like so long ago now, but also no time at all.

I still don't understand why Lieutenant Agkar chose me in the first place. He doesn't want to use me—at least not in *that* way. Neither does he hurt or punish me. Agkar's never been cruel, even when I accidentally spilled some stew on his lap. He just growled in annoyance at my clumsiness and made me clean it up. If anything, he's almost... kind to me. It's in small gestures, like fishing a twig out of my hair when I've been out looking for plants or checking on a wound after I poke myself while sewing.

But that's all. The rest of the time he's closed-off and severe, and barely talks to me. Sometimes, when Agkar's asleep, I cry silently in my bed. I think of Blizzek's face, of the way he felt inside me, how it felt like my heart was tearing in half when he left me.

I miss my home. Arri. Potato. My own bed.

But this is my station now, probably for as long as I live.

One night, while I try to stifle my sobs, I hear Agkar move. I quickly hide under my blankets to muffle the noise—but soon he's stalking toward my bed.

"Stop it," Agkar says gruffly. "I can't sleep."

"I'm sorry. I didn't mean to bother you." After months of serving him, my Trollkin has improved dramatically. He doesn't teach me, per se—not the way that Blizzek did, with such intention—but he does repeat words to make sure I learn them.

Agkar growls and peels back my blankets, and a gust of cold air hits me. I try to pull them back up because I don't like how exposed I am underneath in just my underclothes, but he won't let me.

"Get up," he says, roughly. Have I gotten so far under the Lieutenant's skin this time that his cold shell has cracked?

I do what I'm told and stand up. He grabs me by the arm and starts to drag me across the tent... Right toward his own bed.

"No!" I pull back as hard as I can. "I'm sorry. I won't do it again. Please, don't!"

"Shut up," he snarls. I'm no match for an orc as far as raw strength is concerned, so he simply picks me up under his arm and carries me over to his bed. He tosses me down on it, and I try to scramble away.

"Stop," he growls again. "You're so loud. The point of this is to shut you up."

I know I can't escape, so I cover my mouth and try to swallow my sobs. Maybe if I'm quiet, he won't do it. He lies down on the bed next to me, and my breath is coming so hard and fast that I worry I'm going to pass out. "You need to breathe," he says, forcing me to lie down. "I'm not going to do whatever you're thinking."

Then what am I here for? I try to stop shaking, to stop gasping for air. Maybe if I'm still, this will all end.

"There we go," Agkar says and sighs deeply. He wraps his arms around me, then pulls me in so my face is leaned against his collar. "Your orc isn't here, but I am. So just quiet down. I need my sleep."

Is he trying to comfort me?

The panic starts to subside, and in its place, I feel something like relief. Perhaps Agkar smells quite different than Blizzek did, but his hot skin and dense, hard muscles still remind me of him. I remember falling asleep on Blizzek's shoulder on the floor, feeling that finally, everything was right.

Suddenly the hole he's left in me becomes a gaping chasm—one that will never, ever be filled. It yawns open, impassable. How long can I possibly keep going on without him?

It feels like some part of me has died.

"Agkar," I say quietly. "Why... why did you pick me? And why have you been kind to me?" I just want to understand what I owe him now, what the terms of our agreement are.

He doesn't reply for a long time, and I thought certainly he's fallen asleep already. But then he speaks.

"It was your hands." In the darkness, his voice is still hard, but quieter, the words meant only for my ears. "I watched you work your healer magic, and I decided those hands should not go to waste."

I consider thanking him, but what would I be thanking him for? For keeping us captive? For using me this way? For showing me a few droplets of kindness while I live at his whim?

So I say nothing instead. Slowly, Agkar's breathing evens out, and I join him in sleep.

Blizzek

Where would they have taken her? I imagine it was trollkin scouts who discovered her homestead out here. Just the thought fills me with such fury and grief that I could rip a troll's head right off at the neck.

No. I have to be rational about this. That's what I do, isn't it? Raz was the emotional one, and I'm the rational one. I try to shove down the rage pumping through my blood and make a plan. Where would they have taken her?

Right. The town—the one they're rebuilding on top of graves. While I was shuffled with my unit from place to place as needed, there's no reason to transport meaningless human prisoners. She'll be close to here.

There's another small meow by my feet, and I kneel down to pick up little Arri.

"You're coming with me," I say to him. "We're going to find her."

I find a bag in the house and put the cat inside it, then I'm off. He fights at first but soon realizes it won't get him anywhere, so he falls quiet. "There we go, bud."

Right away I head in the direction of the town. It's been renamed to something like Gagzen, and when I reach the edge, a guard high up in a guard tower waves at me to stop.

"What's your business?" she calls down.

I hold up the bag. "Delivery."

After consulting with the other guard, she starts to twist the pulley controlling the huge wooden gate. And then I'm inside.

The town is bustling with activity. It's more than just soldiers here now—there are civilians of all sorts setting up shops, hawking wares, building homes. Settlers fill their wagons with supplies. The war might have been a stalemate, but the trollkin won something here. We have a solid foothold in the human lands now.

As I walk, I search for signs of prisoners. There are some cages on the far end of town, but they lie empty. No, I need to see where the work is going on. That's where I'll find her.

I head in the direction of some unfinished buildings. Now that the perimeter is complete and the conscripted like me have been released, it's left up to prisoners and day laborers to finish the work we began. When I imagine my Nera, the quiet healer with soft hands, forced to labor morning to night in this heat, I'm overcome with guilt, hatred, and self-loathing. I remember the way the trollkin in charge would whip the pris-oners, and I can't help picturing her beautiful bronze skin riddled with welts and scars.

I will kill anyone who's laid hands on her.

A few trollkin give me funny looks as I head to the other end of town, where construction is heavily underway. There are three lines of prisoners, all chained together at the ankle, working hard under the beating sun. I search their faces for those doe-like brown eyes. But I don't see her.

If she's not here, where could she be? Relocated to another camp, perhaps? I'll have to check every single one until I find her.

"What's your business?" An annoyed troll approaches me. "This area isn't for civilians."

"I'm not a civilian." I gesture to the bag over my shoulder containing Arri. "I have some... Special supplies."

One important thing I learned while conscripted: Soldiers have one very specific enjoyment: the green. They weren't quiet about using it, either. The dark green liquid, squeezed from fresh Syra plants, has a very potent effect when turned into crystals—it quiets the muscles and the mind and replaces your misery with bliss.

Immediately the troll knows what I mean. "Very well," he says and gestures off in the direction of the military encampment.

With a hasty nod, I follow the line of his hand toward the assembled tents. This was a good distraction for now, but I have to leave promptly. There's another town a good thirty miles away that was recently rebuilt; perhaps they reallocated some resources there.

A big orc steps out of one of the tents, a lieutenant's insignia on his chest. He must be the one in charge here. The last thing I need is someone in a position of power questioning what I'm doing here, so I abruptly pivot and head away, back to the main thoroughfare intended for civilian use.

"What's that you've got there?" the orc calls out to me.

I quickly turn around and offer a smile. "I got lost," I say. "It's just rice."

"Big bag for rice." He immediately looks suspicious. "Come over here, orc."

I swallow. Just what I don't need right now is questioning. But if I refuse, that will only raise the alarm, and then I'll really never get out of here.

So I approach him and try to look as flustered and confused as possible. "I didn't mean to trespass," I say.

"Show me what's in the bag." He's the lieutenant here, by his insignia, and he isn't falling for my playing dumb. "Now."

With a sigh, I hold it out and untie the top. When he leans forward to peer inside...

Arri comes leaping out, howling like a banshee. He lands right on the orc's face, burying his claws in his flesh.

"Agh!" The lieutenant flails, desperately reaching for the cat attached to his head. Damn it. Arri might have just sealed his own fate.

"What is it?!" a familiar voice calls out. Someone rushes out of his tent. She's small, far too small for an orcess.

I would know those round cheeks anywhere. Those big, soulful eyes. The long braid hanging over her shoulder.

My Nera.

Her eyes go huge as she registers exactly what's happening: Arri is clinging to the lieutenant's face, and the orc is roaring like a bear as he tries to remove his attacker.

"Wait!" Nera calls out. "Agkar, stop!" She runs toward us, and at that moment, she sees me. Everything in her face goes slack, and her body freezes mid-step.

"Blizzek?" Then her eyes jump back to her cat, who still refuses to let go. One of the other trollkin captains is approaching with a knife, ready to pry Arri right off the lieutenant's face. "No!" She runs for him and puts a hand on the lieutenant's shoulder. "Agkar, please. It's all right."

My blood turns burning hot. Why is she using his name? And why is she *touching him?*

When Arri hears her voice, the cat immediately relaxes. His claws retract as she reaches for him, and suddenly, the lieutenant is free. The cat starts to crawl all over her, meowing like I've never heard him meow.

"What the fuck is going on?" The lieutenant glares at me, then at Nera, and then especially at the cat. He's bleeding from multiple places on his face and neck. He reaches for Arri, but Nera backs away. It takes everything I have not to walk out in front of her, to shove this other orc flat on his back and beat his ugly face to a pulp.

But I stay put. The last thing I need right now is to act rashly toward one of the higher-ups, the military brass. No, I need to keep the attention off of me and her, until I can formulate a plan for getting her out of here.

"Wait. Please." Nera brings the cat to her chest and shows she's not letting him go anytime soon. "He's mine."

At this, the lieutenant pauses. "Yours?" When he turns to face me, and a new look has come over him—suspicion, recognition, and anger, all at once. "Who are you, orc?"

What I really want to know is why my Nera was inside this tent. With a measured voice, I say, "Blizzek." I don't look right at her because I don't need this orc to know we're acquainted.

"And Blizzek," Agkar says slowly, "how did you come by this creature?" He gestures at Arri, who remains purring in Nera's arms.

"I found it," I say. "Out in a house in the woods."

"And you brought it with you, why?"

I shrug, pretending that I don't have a care in the world. "Dinner," I say.

Nera gasps and holds Arri closer to her chest. She's glaring daggers at me. I have no way to explain that I don't mean it—of course, I would never eat her beloved cat—but I have to make this Agkar believe me.

"Hmm." He turns to Nera and fixates on her face. "If the cat is important to her, then it will not be dinner."

That's when I see it: He cares about her. It's plain as day.

Suddenly, everything inside me tightens, winding up into a taut, deadly cord. She came out of his tent, and now he's looking at her like she's his prized possession. Red-hot rage starts to boil up inside me.

Has this damned orc been fucking my mate?

Before I can stop myself, my fist winds back and smashes into the lieutenant's face. He shouts and reels back, clearly taken by surprise. I lunge again, and before he's able to bring up his arms and defend himself, I land yet another fist.

Other military officers are quickly advancing toward us, but I find I can't control my fury. "Wait! Blizzek!" I hear Nera calling after me. "Stop!" Though the lieutenant is blocking, I find my way around and bring up my knee to smash him right in the stomach. He stumbles back and gags. Once more Nera calls my name. "Blizzek, please stop! It's not what you think!"

These last few words return the breath to my lungs. But before I can act, two other military officers have grabbed hold of me. One kicks me in the back, which sends me down to my knees. The other grabs a rope and ties it around my wrists.

When I look up at Nera, there are pools of tears in her eyes. I'm so grateful to see her alive that I don't even mind that they lead me away, Lieutenant Agkar cursing after me.

NERA

When I carry Arri back into Agkar's tent, he quickly leaps out of my arms and makes himself at home on my bed in the corner.

My mind is racing a mile a second. Blizzek is here. Did he come looking for me? Why now? And at what cost?

I wish he hadn't done it. This could all have gone very differently if he had just controlled himself. My stubborn, bull-headed orc. What was he thinking? My stomach is in knots as I remember the guards dragging Blizzek off to a jail cell.

Agkar is clutching his wounds as he enters the tent, and I set immediately to treating them. I draw his hands away from his face and bring up a wet cloth to the little scratches all down his cheeks and neck.

"That creature of yours is a monster," he snarls as I dab each scratch. "Maybe I should eat it."

"Please don't eat him." I switch to the other side of his head. "He's skin and bones. Nothing good there."

Agkar falls silent for a while as I work on him. Finally, he says, "That was him, wasn't it? Your orc?"

All I can do is nod. My Blizzek. The one who walked out on me that day, leaving me naked on my bed. The tears are coming back, but I've gotten good at blinking them away. It's harder this time now that his face is fresh in my mind.

Why is he here? And why did he have Arri with him?

Agkar doesn't speak, but he watches me with keen interest as I clean up his wounds and rub them over with salve, then sit down on my bed. Arri immediately climbs into my lap.

"He's here for you," Agkar says. "And now he's in the brig."

Is he here for me? Maybe it was just a coincidence, but after the way Blizzek went into a rage... I pull Arri close and press my face in his fur. My orc came back. Does that mean he feels the same way I do?

Agkar is just studying me curiously as the tears start to run down my face.

"He means so much to you," the lieutenant says thoughtfully, voice tinged with melancholy. "And clearly, you do to him, as well."

"I don't know about that," I say. "He's the one who left me."

Agkar's eyebrows go up at this. "So he rescinded his claim on you? Then why has he returned?"

I shrug. "I don't know." I can't imagine why it would have taken him a year and more to decide to return for me. It's far too late now.

Agkar gets up and starts to pace. "I should have him hanged for what he did."

At this, my tears return two-fold. Why would Blizzek do something so stupid? I wish he'd have just listened to me.

I remember how Agkar had held me that night when I couldn't stop crying. Perhaps I'm only a slave, but I wonder if I can help Blizzek—negotiate a better punishment for him.

"I'm sorry he did that to you," I say. "But please, don't kill him."

"I won't." I look up at Agkar's words. "I wouldn't be able to stand all your crying."

The relief is sweet. My mouth tilts up into a smile. "Thank you."

"That's not to say he won't die anyway." Agkar narrows his eyes and looks toward the rack of weapons sitting in the corner of his tent. My heart falls into my feet. "But that's up to him."

BLIZZEK

Blizzek, stop! It's not what you think!

How could it not be?

That's what I keep turning over in my mind as two guards drag me away from the scene of my crime. I assaulted a superior officer—a lieutenant, no less—for no ostensible reason. "He's fucking my human mate" is not really an acceptable excuse.

That miserable orc probably forced her, and just thinking this, I want to turn around and beat the tar out of him all over again. I want to cut off his head and mount it on a spike.

I'm furious at myself for leaving in the first place. All of this could have been avoided if I had stayed that day, or taken her away with me instead.

I will never leave her side again, no matter what they try to do to me.

I'm dragged inside the ramshackle jail and hurled into a

cell. The door slams closed behind me. "Get your head on straight," one of the guards growls. "Lunatic."

And then I'm left alone to my devices. Hours pass, and eventually, I'm brought some watery slop to eat. I wonder what the lieutenant is doing with my little Nera while I sit and waste time in here. Just the thought of it makes me seethe. I get up and rattle the bars.

"Hey!" I shout. "What are you going to do with me?"

But nobody answers. I probably won't be sentenced to death for what I did, but years behind bars would be just as bad knowing that Nera's out there, being held by another orc against her will.

Then, the door to the jail opens, and a guard walks in. He stops in front of my cell.

"It's your lucky day," he says, twisting the key in the door. "You've just been given your chance to go free."

"What?" It can't be that easy. There's no way. Besides, I'm not going anywhere without Nera.

"Lieutenant Agkar has challenged you to a Narzag-kig." The guard swings the door open and hands me a sword. It's rusty at the edges.

A fight to the death.

"Over what?" I ask. No one invokes the Narzag-kig for a simple fistfight. No, it's a challenge—usually saved for only the greatest of insults, for the ownership of a prized possession, or to choose between two romantic matches.

The guard looks just as mystified as I feel. "Ownership of the human slave," he says. "Not sure why she's so important to the two of you, though. Seems like a stupid waste of life to me."

So that's it. Agkar wants her as much as I do, does he? He must deeply underestimate me, to be willing to put it all on the line for a slave. And he must care about her an immense amount, too.

I pick up the sword and lick my lips. Very well. I'll happily fight for my mate. I'll either kill him and win, or die trying.

NERA

A Narzag-kig. From Agkar's description, it's a call to battle, winner takes all—including the loser's life. And he's challenging Blizzek, but for what?

"You." Agkar takes an axe off the wall and twirls it in his hand, testing it.

Me? "Why?" I ask. I'm just a slave, and Agkar's putting his life on the line to what, claim ownership of me? "Let him go. You don't need to fight him."

He sets the axe back down and picks up a mace. Just the sight of it invokes the sound of bones crunching, and I cringe.

"By attacking me, he asserted his claim over you," he says. "It makes me look weak to step aside and let the wheels of justice take care of him."

"Then look weak." I gently tug on his cloak, but he just hangs the mace up again and ignores me. "Please. Don't kill him."

This time, Agkar settles on a sword. He balances it on his index finger, then swoops up the handle in his hand.

"You don't have much faith in this orc, do you?" Agkar chuckles at that, turning around to face me. "You're more afraid for him than you are for me."

No, I've seen how resilient Blizzek is—I've cleaned his battle scars. But I can't even risk it. If he were to die in front of me... I don't think I could survive that.

Seeing my expression, Agkar leans close and looks down

into my eyes. "You care for him so much," he says. "That's why I have to win."

"To kill the one person I treasure most?" I back away from him, feeling a new, fresh anger. "And what about you? What if he wins?" I don't want to see Agkar killed either, not over *me*.

His face softens, and he brings up a hand to my cheek. "You worry about me?"

"There's just no reason for anyone to die in this!"

"Yes, there is." He releases me, but his eyes stay fixed on my face. "Once he's dead, you'll have to forget about him eventually. And then you'll be all mine."

He turns away and throws open the door flaps, carrying his sword up against one shoulder.

He's mistaken if he thinks he can simply erase Blizzek. "I'll never forget," I say in a low voice to his back.

Agkar just grunts. "We will see about that."

Outside the tent, trollkin have already started gathering around in a wide circle, kicking up clouds of dust with their anticipation. When Agkar steps into the ring, a cheer goes up from the assembled recruits. He drops the tip of the sword into the dirt and leans against the hilt like he doesn't have a care in the world. Someone whoops.

Then, from the other end of the camp, two guards escort Blizzek toward us. He carries a sword as well—a significantly smaller one. He has quite a bit less armor than Agkar does, too. They must have taken his chainmail when they put him behind bars. It's deeply unfair.

I breathe hard out and then in again. I need to have faith in him.

As they bring him into the ring, Blizzek searches for me. There. His bright amber eyes lock on mine, and I can't look away.

Mine, I can almost hear him saying. I recognize that look.

He's not planning to lose. He can't possibly because, in that look, I know everything that he feels.

Shame. Guilt. Devotion. He didn't want to leave. He came back here for me, brought Arri to me. He wants me as much as I want him. But why now?

Blizzek turns away then and rubs one of his tusks. He seems different immediately—self-assured, almost arrogant. He walks up to where Agkar is standing and gets right in his face.

"All of this? Over one human female?" Blizzek barks a laugh. I know he doesn't mean it. He's trying to get Agkar riled up, but I don't think it will work. The lieutenant is too collected to fall for that.

"I know you've chosen her as your mate," Agkar says. The assembled trollkin fall quiet at this. "And you want her back."

But Blizzek chuckles to himself. "You overestimate," he says. "She was a convenient hole for me. That's all."

Agkar's mouth twists, his snarl like a tiger's. "Then it will be easy to make her forget about you when you're gone," he says. "And she can be all mine."

Murmurs spread through the crowd as it becomes clear they aren't just fighting over a slave. No, they're fighting for mating rights—to a human.

Blizzek scowls at this. His bluff has been called. "Fine," he grunts. "I guess I'll just have to kill you first. Then I get to leave here alive and one human slave richer."

There's no gunshot to signal the start of the fight. Blizzek simply leaps, sword outstretched. But Agkar is prepared and parries his first attack with a snort of derision. The audience crows.

"That's all you've got?" The lieutenant swipes, and Blizzek blocks it just in time. They dance around one another, and I'm amazed at how quick and agile they both are for being so tall and built as thick as old growth trees. Blizzek is a skilled fighter, managing to glance a blow off of Agkar's chest plate while the other orc gets in nothing.

But Blizzek also still favors his injured side, and I think Agkar has noticed. He dives for the weakness and manages to slip through, slicing across Blizzk's hip. It's just a surface wound, but I cover my mouth and clutch my side because it's like I can feel his injury in my own body. The crowd cheers.

With a laugh, Blizzek spins away and uses the opening to swipe with one leg, driving Agkar to his knees. Then he slashes again, and the loud *clang!* of their weapons rings out as Agkar blocks just in time. Agkar is younger, but Blizzek fights dirty. I have hope.

And then once more, Agkar slips through Blizzek's defenses. This time, his sword gets Blizzek across the thigh, and my orc lets out a guttural roar.

I have to help him, but there's nothing I can do.

CHAPTER 15

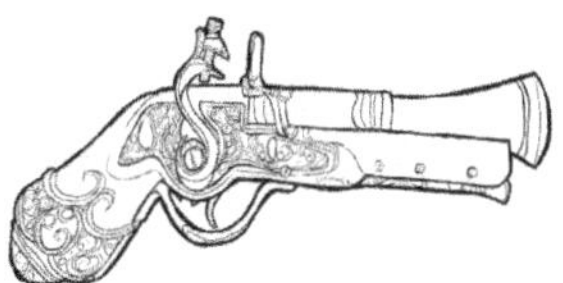

At this rate, I'm going to bleed out. I have to end this quickly.

While that bastard lieutenant is gloating over his victory, I push off with my good thigh and dive toward his right side. I have to give this Agkar fellow credit for being quick, because he responds right away, twisting to the other side to block my attack. I expected this—he's a strong fighter, but a simpleminded one. A soldier.

Instead, I swipe in the other direction and drive the point of my sword right into his side. A gasp rises up from the crowd as it sinks in deep. Then I yank my sword back out, and blood starts to pour out of him.

There. That does it.

I don't even give him a moment to recover. I stab again, this time catching him in the arm between his armor plates. Bleeding, Agkar stumbles away.

"Damn it," he hisses, but he doesn't go down. So I lunge

again, and instead of using my sword, I drive an elbow right into his other side. He groans and tries to dodge, but he's too slow now. I deliver an uppercut to his jaw, and in one motion Agkar, the decorated lieutenant of the Great Chieftain's army, falls to his knees.

It's over. All I have to do is cut off his head, and then Nera and I can walk out of here alive.

"Wait!" I turn at the sound of her voice. She's rushing into the arena, waving her arms in front of me. All around us, trollkin start to shout and jeer. They don't care anymore who's winning or who's losing, they just want to see blood pour.

Nera stands in front of Agkar. "Nera," I say. "Stand out of the way."

"Please. Don't kill him."

Does she not understand that this is the Narzag-kig? He challenged me. It's his fate to die.

"That is how it goes." I take another step toward him.

"It doesn't have to." When she looks at me, I can see all the kindness and empathy and generosity in her eyes, the things that leave me in awe of her. "You won, didn't you?"

"We can't go free until he's dead." There's only one way this can possibly end.

Nera turns to Agkar and kneels down in front of him. I bristle all over. Does she care for him, too? "Say you give up," she tells him.

"Never." The idiot orc even starts to stand up, but the gaping wound in his side brings him back down.

"Just say it!" Her voice is suddenly large and strong, and angry. "Admit you lost! I don't want you to die!"

It feels as if no one is breathing. This small human who speaks Trollkin, who interferes in a Narzag-kig, is telling a lieutenant what to do.

Have I returned too late, and I've already lost her?

Agkar raises his head, and there's a twinge of a smile on his face. "What, so you do worry about me, after all?"

"Of course I do!" Now I really want to kill him. "As I do for every creature that lives. There's no reason for you to die here. Just... just let me go, Agkar. Please."

The arena is silent as the lieutenant considers her. It's blasphemous, for a Narzag-kig to end in surrender. It would be the most dishonorable victory possible for me.

But I'm already mated to a human. I don't really have much pride to stand on anymore, do I? And right now she's so fierce and gentle and perfectly Nera that I find I don't want to be the one to kill him, not in front of her.

"Fine." Agkar clutches his side. "I admit defeat."

Jeers and boos go up from the crowd. Then trollkin start to move toward us, and they close in. They wanted blood and they're going to get it.

"It's the human's fault," one says.

I hold up my sword and stand in front of her. "If you touch her, I kill you." They've already seen what I can do, so they hesitate.

"Stand down," a pained voice says. Slowly, Agkar drags himself back up to his feet, clutching his side. "I said I admitted defeat, didn't I?"

"But sir, the Narzag-kig...!" someone says.

"Stand down!" His roar echoes across the camp, and all the trollkin fall still.

"You need help," Nera says. She glances at one of the guards and summons him over—too surprised to object, the guard obeys. "Take him back to his tent and get my supplies."

"Nera." When I say her name, my human falls still. Then she turns to me, face red, but relieved. I feel like I could drown in her. "I'm sorry," I say to her, my voice husky. "I'm so sorry I left."

She reaches out and takes my hand in hers. "I know," she says, winding our fingers together. "I forgive you."

Just like that. What did I ever do to deserve this little human?

I don't care who's watching—I just need to feel her again. So I wrap my arms tight around her waist and pull her in. Gasps go up from the crowd as I lean down and seize her mouth in mine.

NERA

He won. Blizzek won.

His lips taste like everything I've ever wanted, everything I've been dreaming of since the day he walked out. I sink into his chest, and he pulls me even closer, so tight against him that I wonder if we'll simply merge into a single person.

Over the audible surprise and distress of our trollkin audience, one whoop goes up into the air. Then another, and another, as we continue to put on a show for them.

If they can't have blood, at least they'll have entertainment.

Eventually, I have to pull away because there's a patient who needs attending. Blizzek looks confused as I step back from him.

"I'm sorry," I say. "I have to make sure that Agkar's all right and treat his wound. It is very severe."

A frown crosses his face. "He already surrendered. It's time for us to go."

But I can't leave like this. The lieutenant was already losing blood quickly—and there's no healer in this town who could help except for me. Blizzek's wounds will be easy to clean and bandage, but Agkar could bleed to death unless I see to him.

"I know," I tell him softly. "But I have to do this." Blizzek's confusion slowly recedes, and soon I find understanding in his amber eyes.

"That's just who you are, isn't it?" He pushes some hair back behind my ear. Then he leans down, so close to my face that his tusk scrapes my cheek. "Just one of the many reasons you're my mate."

His breath tickles my ear, and suddenly my entire body is warm and ready for him. He could take me right now, right here in the middle of the camp, and I would let him. It ripples through me all at once, and Blizzek chuckles. "Go, then. I'll have you later."

I clear my throat and step away, and the trollkin boo at us. The show is over.

Inside Agkar's tent, there are dribbles of blood all along the floor. He lies on his bed gasping for air as I approach him.

"Why are you here?" he snarls. "You've chosen."

"Stop it." I pull out my supplies and walk over to him, kneeling down by the bed to get a better look at his wounds. "And let me do my job."

As ordered, he falls silent.

After cleaning the wounds thoroughly—at which Agkar lies as still and silent as a stone—I stitch it up and then rub salve around the skin. The blood slowly stops flowing, and I step back to look over my work.

Agkar stares at the wall. He's obviously humiliated, twice over now.

"I should be dead," he says.

"Now you'll live instead. You can die some other time." I pack everything up into my basket again. Agkar doesn't say another word to me as I exit the tent, where outside, Blizzek is waiting. The crowd has mostly dispersed, but soldiers still stand around staring at us.

"We should leave town," Blizzek says. "Before they change their minds about letting us live."

But I just shake my head. I have a patient to look after. "When Agkar's well, we can go wherever you like." I gesture to his thigh. "Besides, I think you're in need of some attention, too."

All it takes is one look at my face for Blizzek to sigh and nod in submission. "Fine. If that's what you really want."

My bull-headed orc.

Blizzek

My huge-hearted woman.

I want her so badly that I'm willing to pay whatever ridiculous price they're asking at this filthy horse stable that calls itself an inn. Word has already traveled to the civilian side of town about the fight between me and the lieutenant. There's the orc who almost paid his life for a human slave.

Oh, and then kissed her in front of everyone.

I couldn't give a rat's ass. I want nothing more than to get her naked on the bed, saying my name.

When we're upstairs, I pull her inside and slam the door closed. I wrap her up as tight as I possibly can, but before I can kiss her, she's kissing me first and I groan into her mouth. Tasting her again is like going back to the place I grew up, and seeing all the familiar things that have made me what I am.

But then, she gently pulls away.

"Sit down," Nera says, gesturing to the bed. It's straw

loosely wrapped in canvas. She takes out the basket of supplies, with Arri still sleeping inside.

"I'm fine," I say as she starts to pull out her various solutions. "They're surface wounds."

"Do you really think you can fight me on this and win?"

I have to grin at her stern tone, but I obey and sit down. "Your Trollkin is good," I say.

Her own smile falters a little. "I've been here a long time."

All the pleasure I felt vanishes. Everything that happened here today, that's happened since the day I left, is my fault. I don't think I could ever make it up to her.

"What did he do to you?" I ask quietly. I don't want to know the answer, but I feel like I need to. What horrors have I put her through by abandoning her?

But Nera just shakes her head. "Nothing. He did nothing."

I'm genuinely surprised by this. That big, arrogant orc didn't touch her? I'm so relieved that I could pull her into my arms right then, but I know I have to wait until she's done with her work.

"I'm so glad." Not that learning this information makes up for all the other horrors she's experienced since she was taken prisoner. "I'm sorry, Nera. I was a huge fool. The biggest of them all."

She doesn't say anything for a long time, simply focused on my wounds. Then, without looking up she says, "Why?"

I know exactly what she's asking. Why did I leave that day, with her naked on the bed? I took her heart, put it on the ground, and smashed it to pieces. No—I did it to both of us.

"I was afraid." I felt so many powerful things when I was with her, and all of them scared me. I thought I was broken. I thought she would be better off without me. "I believed I was doing the right thing by not being in your life."

She sits back on her knees and considers me. She's always

so patient, so thoughtful, so in touch with herself that I'm envious.

"You know now that's not true?" she asks.

I quickly nod. "Everything is wrong without you." Once she's finished, I take her hand and pull her up onto the bed beside me. "You are my mate, I know that now, and I can't go on living unless you're by my side."

Nera puts one hand on my face and leans forward until our foreheads are touching. I'm longing to tear off her clothes, to show her exactly what it means to be mine, but I force myself to wait.

"Don't ever leave me again," she says.

I nod hastily. "I would never."

She smiles then, and I pull her in for a kiss. Her mouth is just as hungry as mine, and we devour each other. I can feel her need in this kiss, and soon, I have to pull away because the urge is almost too powerful for me to control. Her eyes travel from my face, down to my chest, and then to the massive boner in my lap. She grins mischievously.

"Still so hard for me," she whispers and reaches down to touch it. I shudder and groan at the mere ghost of her fingers over my leather pants.

"Always," I say. "From the very first moment." I remember how she leaned over me as she cleaned my wounds, and her big breasts are just as tantalizing now as they were then. She'll be able to feed lots of whelps with them, I think.

Suddenly I understand my friend much better.

I can barely stand her hands on me—I might even let one off inside my pants if she continues—so I gently move them away and reach for the hem of her shirt. She's been dressed in orcish clothes and furs, and I have to admit that I like them on her. It's almost as if she's one of us.

Seeing her body again fills me with an unparalleled elation, a hope for the future I thought had been snuffed out. Her brown nipples are already hard as pebbles, and when I take one in my mouth, she gasps. It's been so long since I heard her little pleasure sounds, but now, I'll never be without them again. I'll make her moan like this forever.

Once I take her pants off, my hands cover every inch of her body, all the way down to her five toes. I worship her, dragging my lips down to her ankles and back up again. When she's breathing hard underneath me, I press her back against the bed and kiss my way down her belly, which is almost unbearably thin. It hurts in a deep place as I imagine how she's suffered. I will hunt every single deer for her until she's thick around the middle again.

I pull her legs apart, and Nera lets out a little gasp of surprise as I bring my mouth down between them. She smells like everything I've been dreaming of, like woods and sweat, and her own perfect musk. I'm going to make her come so many times, she won't be able to move.

Chapter 16

Nera

Blizzek knows exactly what he's doing with his tongue. He traces my folds, drawing circles closer and closer to my clit until finally, he brushes over it. It's just a feather touch, but it makes me clench. I can feel his hot breath on me, soaking me up, breathing me in.

And then he goes to work. It's only a few seconds before I'm moaning. The way he tantalizes my nub, and then ducks down to brush against my entrance and back again is driving me into a frenzy. Just when I think I'm about to burst, he gently slides a finger inside me and starts to suck hard on my clit. It only takes a few strokes of his fingertip against my inner wall to break me, and I can feel the explosion inside and outside. I simply gush over him, like a dam has broken.

"Incredible," Blizzek whispers and drinks me up. He licks his lips but doesn't remove his finger from me. I'm so tight that I'm not sure if he could.

That's when a second finger squeezes inside me. I don't

know how it fits but it does, and then he starts moving again, alternating each one as he continues to lap me up. I might not survive this.

"I'm going to get you good and ready," he whispers as he looks up over my mound of dark hair and locks eyes with me. "So ready for me."

Just the sound of his voice drives me over the edge again, and I cry out. "Ahh," he says, finally withdrawing his hand. "You're so tight. I don't know how I'll ever fit inside you."

I can't say I know how, either—but I'm certain that he will. And how good he'll feel there, right where he belongs.

"You should know now that I'm going to fuck you all night long," he says, rising up so he's crouched over me, one hand on either side of my head. His wounds don't seem to bother him at all. There's a fresh intensity in his eyes, a longing and desire that has been building inside him ever since he left. "I'll start soft, but by the end, you'll be up against the wall and screaming my name."

All I can do is nod because I want the very same thing. With a grunt of approval, Blizzek kisses all the way back up my body to my mouth again. I reach for his cock, because all I want is to feel it in my hands, but he wags a finger at me. "If you touch me, I won't be able to hold out." He leans down closer, his lips only a hair's breadth away from mine. "All I want is you, Nera."

They're the words I needed to hear. His mouth gently settles on mine, and instead of ravaging me like I expected, Blizzek is soft and tantalizing, loving and caring and so patient. I melt into his hands, and he eagerly holds me up.

Then, he decides that it's time, and I'm in complete agreement. He brings his cock between my legs, but doesn't dive in —no, he rubs his head all around me, spreading the moisture he drew out of me when he fucked me with his mouth. I already have my arms wrapped around his neck, bucking my hips against his because all I want is for him to be inside of me.

"You want it?" he whispers into my ear, and all I can do is nod furiously. I want it more than anything.

"Please," I whisper.

"Then you'll have it."

It's lucky that his head is shaped perfectly for prying me open because, at first, it seems like he won't fit. I forgot how big he is, and how much my body has to adjust to prepare for him. But Blizzek is in absolutely no rush. After agonizing minutes of gentle teasing, he slides in like a dream.

"Ah," he says, resting his forehead against mine. "There we are."

"Blizzek," I manage out. "You feel perfect." I know he's going slowly to make me comfortable, and taking his time to show me just how much he's longed for me, but suddenly I want everything. I want it all. I want him to take me hard and show me how fervently he wants me back.

I know he can read all of this off my face because he just smiles and cradles my cheek in his hand. "Soon enough," he says.

When Blizzek is finally seated right where he belongs, I feel whole again. I wrap my legs around his waist and when he starts to move, staying deep and thrusting only a few inches at a time, I feel pressure build in my face. The way he holds me, the way he treats my body like a temple, the way it feels to have him with me again—I can't help the tears that slip free. Blizzek leans forward and kisses each of them away.

"Your heart," he says quietly, still thrusting with perfect, slow precision, "is so wonderful, Nera."

Oh, I don't know how I'll be able to stand it, but stand it I do. Soon I'm begging into his ear for more.

"Is that right?" Blizzek asks playfully. He reaches under my thighs and brings them up to his waist, and that's when he starts to drive into me faster, and harder. Every last thought flees my mind as his wet cock slides in and out, in and out, in a dance as old as time itself. I'm lost to it, and when my next orgasm hits me, I cry his name.

BLIZZEK

Oh, my Nera. My soft, gentle mate, so warm and trusting under my hands.

I will never, ever betray that trust again. I'm going to pleasure this human woman in my arms so many times that she'll never forget it.

I let her recover for just a few moments, and then I gently pull myself free. She lets out a little whimper, but I say, "I promise, I'm staying here all night."

I pull her to her feet and pick her up, and it's like she weighs nothing. Once I have her against the wall and her legs are laced around my waist, I drive into her again, and she's so hot and slick with her own juices that pounding her is easy. As she starts to scream, I capture her lips in mine, shoving her harder and harder against the wall. She moans into my mouth.

"Blizzek," she whispers. "More. More."

And I give her more. I slam into her so hard that my sac is slapping her ass, over and over. When I feel her tighten around me again, her cries growing higher and higher in pitch, I can't hold it in any longer. I'm going to fill her up with everything I have, and when my cock grows engorged inside her, Nera reaches her breaking point. She falls silent as she pulls me in as deep as she possibly can, and I feel her bite down hard on my shoulder.

"Blizzek," she whispers, and her entire channel squeezes tight all around me. Perfect. She won't let any of my seed go to waste like this. It's the most exquisite bliss.

"I'm going to fill you up," I growl into her ear. "I'm going to put so many whelps inside you, my dearest Nera."

I erupt inside her, and she lets out another cry as it draws her climax out even further. I bury myself as deep as I can, and it all spills out of me in one thunderstorm of pleasure. I imagine it filling up her belly, finding a purchase inside her, and starting a new life there. And while she's fat and shining with orc whelps, I'm going to keep fucking her, keep sucking on each of her engorged breasts until I pull the milk out of them.

She will be mine and I'll be hers, over and over until we have a whole little house full of our offspring. I want nothing else.

Nera is panting when I carry her back over to the bed, still deep inside her. I hold her legs up and gently withdraw, making sure as little of my seed pours out of her as possible. She giggles.

"Oh yes?" she asks, face bright red. "You think that will work?"

"I know it will." I realize just how much I have to tell her. "I've seen proof."

When I can't possibly hold myself up any longer, we both fall to the bed. I draw her into me as close as I can, and I feel like I could just swallow her up.

"You're an incredible lover," she says, tracing the lines of my face with her finger. She runs it over my sharp tusks, up to my ears, and through my hair. She turns over one of the bones holding a small braid in place, and I bury my face in her neck.

I'm lucky. I'm so, so lucky. And I'll never forget it.

NERA

We stay up for hours, just talking, reveling in the feel of each other's warm bodies. Blizzek tells me all about his friend Raz'jin, who met and mated with a human of his own.

"Troll babies?" I'm aghast. "I had no idea that could happen."

Blizzek just smirks at me. "He claims it's hard, but I think I can give him a run for his money."

I have to giggle at this, just thinking about what it would be like to bear Blizzek's orc children. What do orc babies look like? Would any of them come out human, instead?

"Peculiar thing," I say. "That we would be made this way. I would never have believed it—me, with an orc. But it's almost like it was meant to be."

"I've thought the very same thing." Blizzek sighs contentedly and kisses the top of my head. "I was drawn to you for a reason. I wonder what that reason is?"

But neither of us has an answer. Eventually, my exhaustion catches up to me, and I fall asleep in his huge, warm arms.

The next morning, I have a patient to attend to. The guards don't stop me when I approach Agkar's tent. He lays on his bed, and when I enter, he looks up to see who's come to disturb him. But when he registers that it's me, he falls back to his furs and says nothing.

I don't blame him. His pride is deeply wounded, and I've discovered that if orcs have anything, it's pride. I check over his wounds, clean them again, and apply a numbing salve to help the pain. Agkar keeps his eyes firmly on the wall as I leave his tent. A heartbroken orc is a sad thing.

Out in the square, trollkin are surprised to see me walking at Blizzek's side. A few soldiers encircle us. "It's time that you and your little slave leave," one of them says, prodding me with the blunt end of a spear. Blizzek grabs the spear and, in one motion, breaks it in half. The soldiers take a few steps back.

Blizzek holds his hands up. "Fine. We're going." He takes my hand, and, with Arri in my basket of supplies, we head for the gates. The pulley squeals as it opens, and we step outside.

"Wait." It's a deep, gruff voice that I recognize. It's Agkar, holding his side as he limps toward us. "We need her here."

Blizzek turns around and his eyes are daggers. "You have no claim over her anymore," he snarls. "She is free."

"I know." Agkar isn't talking to him, though—he's looking at me. "We have no healer here. You've been invaluable to our efforts. Many of our soldiers are only alive because of you."

"That's none of our concern," Blizzek says.

But I know that Agkar's right. With conditions here as they are, the sick will continue to pile up. And the other human prisoners... How many of them might die out here?

I shake my head. "I'm sorry, Agkar. As long as my kind are enslaved here, I can't stay."

Blizzek starts walking again, and I'm right along beside him.

"Fine." Agkar rises to his full height. "As the overseeing officer here, the human prisoners can go free."

Trollkin have assembled once again at the gates to the city, and hushed whispers are spreading through the town as Agkar makes his announcement.

"Sir, we won't have enough bodies to finish the wall," one of his soldiers says.

"Then the wall will take longer." Agkar's eyes are focused on mine. "We need the healer more than we need the prisoners."

I can't help but smile. "Then it's a deal."

CHAPTER 17

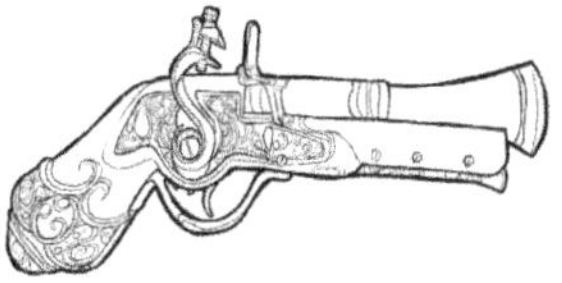

BLIZZEK

That was not how I expected any of this to go.

I almost feel sorry for him, this lieutenant who also fell for my Nera. But I understand easily how it can happen—she is a glimmer of sunshine on a dark, stormy day. We are drawn to her like moths to a flame.

But he's also right. If this village doesn't have a healer, that doesn't bode well for the future as more and more civilians move in. There will be deaths and births, injuries and fights, and everyone could benefit from having a skilled craftswoman like Nera around.

"Then it's a deal." She didn't even ask me what I thought, and it's just fuel to the fire of how much I adore her. She could wrap a chain around my neck and lead me to and fro and I'd do it.

Agkar just nods once, sharply, and turns back the way he came. No one would dare defy him, as much as they want to.

"But I'm not living here," she says. "My house. That's where we'll stay. I don't want anyone to bother us there."

Agkar pauses. "Then that's how it will be," he says and walks away.

When it's settled, I wrap my arm around Nera's waist, and we walk out. The gates fall closed behind us.

"Your house, then?" I say with a wink.

"You don't mind, do you?"

When I look into her brown eyes, I'm willing to do anything. "No, of course not. I love your home." Then I sigh after remembering what I found there. "I'll have to buy you some more sheep, though."

"Maybe they still have Potato." She looks thoughtful. "So much has changed."

I pull her closer as we walk into the woods. "I know. But things will get better, I promise. We'll have a life together right here, on your own land."

Nera smiles widely at this. "I could never have imagined."

Me, settling down on a little farm with a human woman? "Me, neither."

NERA

It takes time, but slowly, we rebuild what the trollkin took and destroyed. Agkar, though he won't see me in person, freely gives us the supplies we need to replant and start over, with the understanding that as our operation grows, we will share produce and meat with the village slowly growing nearby. My healing services will, of course, always be free.

Whenever they're in need of me, the village sends an emissary to collect me. True to his word, Agkar releases the other human prisoners, and soon more day laborers are brought in to replace them.

Blizzek sets about building a fence all the way around the farm, so no encroaching settlers will get any funny ideas. It's strange to see other trollkin from time to time, attending to their own crops and farms and families far off in the woods.

Within a year, we've expanded the garden to three times its previous size and have a lush crop growing in. It's breeding season for the sheep—and for us, too.

You'd think Blizzek would be exhausted after spending the day working the garden, but if anything, he's more alive than ever when the sun sets. We've barely finished eating our dinner when he's leaned over the back of my chair, just nibbling at my earlobe. His mouth moves to my throat, then my collarbone, and soon he's pushing down the sleeve of my shirt so he can get better access to my shoulder.

"Enough," he says brusquely to the shirt, which is clearly getting in his way, and reaches for the bottom instead.

"I'm still at the dinner table!" But I'm laughing as he yanks it upward, over my head, and tosses it to the floor. He drags the chair around so I'm facing him, and kneels down in front of me. His stern amber eyes travel down my chest and then back up to my face.

"You're so beautiful." He picks up my foot and kisses me on each of my five toes, then works his way up my calf and leg. He tugs the hem of my skirt up and pulls me to the front of the chair.

So he's going to have me that way, is he?

He doesn't dive in right away, instead choosing to kiss up the inside of my thigh so I'm breathing a little harder. When he finally reaches the sensitive spot between my legs, his tongue darts out from between his tusks and gently laps at the outside of my folds. He traces every last inch of me with that tongue. My legs are shivering by the time he wraps his lips around my clit and sucks on it, and that makes me moan.

"You like that, do you?" he whispers, and repeats the motion again, and again, until I'm leaning back in the chair and grasping the sides tightly in my fists. He worships me, adding one finger to the mix, until the sparks of pleasure he's been sending into my belly have turned into hot lightning.

"I'm going to come," I whisper as every last muscle in my body tightens. It crests a wave, and suddenly I'm being sucked under, crying out as Blizzek draws out my orgasm as far as it will possibly go until I can't take any more.

When he's finished, I'm shuddering and clenching around him, my body boneless. He stands up and offers me his hand.

I know what comes next, and I want it more than anything.

He leads me back into the bedroom—our bedroom, now—and while I'm still soft and sensitive between the legs, he strips off his clothes and sinks himself deep inside me. I bury my fingers into the thick muscle of his back, and he breathes hard into my neck.

"You always feel so perfect," he says, only sliding out an inch or two before thrusting back in. I know what he's after. That secret place that makes the world fade away around us until all I can feel is him. He holds me tight against his body as he seeks it out, kissing my forehead and nuzzling my hair while he searches.

"I've heard them say," he says between animalistic grunts, "that the more times you make your female orgasm, the more likely she is to get with whelp."

I'm already tightening up underneath him again, coiling like a wind-up toy. Every time he thrusts, his chest brushes my nipples again, and it feels like every inch of me is electrified.

"Surely you'll succeed this time," I manage out between moans.

"Surely I will," he says, just as my climax smashes over me, carrying me out to sea. It's just the first of many that afternoon.

"Tough nut to crack," Blizzek says, rubbing his chin. "I thought I'd have succeeded by now."

I grin from my spot underneath him, his come spilling out of me onto the bed. "You're certainly trying your best."

"I guess I'll have to write to Raz for some tips."

In the second year, though, he manages to land one. It's not long before I'm swelling up big, and he has to help me get to the village and back for my work. One day I spy Agkar watching us pass from his tent, but I can't read his look.

I'm almost ready to burst when one afternoon, there comes a knock at the door.

Blizzek opens it, and his hand falls to the utility knife he keeps at his hip when he sees a human woman standing outside. But she just barges inside, ignoring him completely.

"You must be Nera!" She runs toward me, and before I know it, I'm being hugged by a complete stranger. When she pulls away, she laughs. "Oops, sorry. I should introduce myself. I'm Telise."

It dawns on me—Raz'jin's human mate. She eyes my gigantic belly.

"Yup. Looks familiar." She shoots a glare at Blizzek. "She should be resting, you know. Carrying little baby orcs and trolls is not an easy business for us."

"Oh." He's in shock still, so I lead Telise out of the living room.

"I'm here to help!" she says brightly. "And also to hunt. There are these alligators who live way out here, and I desperately want one."

"As a pet?" I ask.

"No, silly. I'm gonna make the best pair of boots you've ever seen."

Our quiet home becomes a whirlwind of activity as Telise makes her presence known. But as the whelp inside me gets bigger and bigger, I'm grateful that she's here.

I'm especially grateful when it decides it's time to come out.

BLIZZEK

I have never heard a worse sound than Nera's screams.

Shit. Maybe I shouldn't have done this after all. But she just holds onto my hand tight as Raz'jin's annoying little mate crouches down between Nera's legs.

"Just a bit more! I see it!" Nera cries out again, and I drape a cool cloth on her forehead. She's working so hard, and I just have to sit here and do nothing. It's agonizing.

And then, right when I think I can't tolerate any more of it —Nera gasps with relief, and a sharp, bright cry fills the house.

"Oh," says Telise, looking down at the wet baby in her arms with surprise. "You got a different one than I did."

"A different one?" I ask, perplexed. She holds out a little golden-skinned creature that is, most definitely, human. At first, I'm repulsed—it looks so fragile and small—but the moment I have it in my arms, it's like I've been turned inside-out. Her tiny eyes open, and when I see just how deep and brown they are, my heart stops beating.

She's wonderful.

"Let me see her," Nera says. I hand the infant over reluctantly. "Five fingers and toes. No green skin." She grins at me as she brings the little thing to her breast. "And all us."

A few days later, Telise is packing up her things to go. "Well, if you decide to try for another one, let me know what comes out, will you?"

With that, she's gone, and I'm grateful it can just be the three of us in our little home together.

The baby grows fast, and Arri bonds to her right away. Sometime in the first month, a gift is sent from the village: Candies imported from Kalishagg. There's no name attached, but I know who it's from.

But I never have to worry. We've hung up the painting of Nera and her former mate, Refiel, so that she doesn't forget him. I know she cares for me more than anyone in the world— except maybe the little girl we made.

I sit at the table, whittling some wood into what I hope will become a toy if I can just get the edges softened out. Nera is helping Zarie walk across the floor.

"She's getting so good at this." Nera has started growing big and round again. I'm quite excellent at my job—better than Raz'jin, at least. I wonder if this time, it'll come out looking like me.

Sure, the trollkin find us strange, and for the most part, they leave us alone to our devices. That's all I want anyway: To be left alone with my family and our little farm out in the woods.

If you enjoyed the book, please consider leaving a review! Reviews help indie authors like me find new readers.

WHAT TO READ NEXT

Discover what becomes of Lieutenant Agkar in the next book in the Trollkin Lovers series, *Capturing the Orc's Heart*!

JOIN MY NEWSLETTER!

For all the latest regarding books, and to get a FREE Trollkin Lovers novelette, join my newsletter!

www.LyonneRiley.com

About the Author

Lyonne Riley published her first book at age five, which was written on tiny sheets of notebook paper, and she insisted on giving a copy to everyone she knew. She's been writing ever since, from fan fiction in her teen years to original fiction as an adult. After a stint in traditional publishing, she discovered what she truly wanted to write: very smutty stories about monstrous trolls and the little humans they worship.

Now she lives in the middle of nowhere with her dogs and spouse, writing sexy fairy tales.

facebook.com/lyonneriley

x.com/lyonneriley

instagram.com/lyonneriley

amazon.com/stores/Lyonne-Riley/author/B0C57K1NM3

Acknowledgments

I would like to thank everyone involved in helping me through the process of putting out my second self-published book. This was a rocky road, and I can't say enough how much I appreciate the help and encouragement of the people around me. Thank you to Amber for suggesting I do this in the first place. Huge thanks to my cover artist, Rowan Woodcock, who brought Blizzek and Nera to life. Thank you to my critique partners, especially Ruth, who give me phenomenal editorial feedback: You all make this possible. And of course, my amazing spouse, who has always supported my dreams—and given me lots of inspiration for my characters' sexy adventures.

I couldn't have done this without the expertise of my fellow self-published romance authors, Chace Verity and Pamela DuMond. Thank you for inviting me into your circles and helping me through this process.

And thank you to my readers, who gave this book a shot.

www.ingramcontent.com/pod-product-compliance
Lightning Source LLC
Chambersburg PA
CBHW060746210726

48292CB00015B/2807